Morris Gleitzman

Sticky Beak

**MACMILLAN
CHILDREN'S BOOKS**

First published 1993 by Pan Macmillan Publishers Australia

First published in the UK 1994 by Macmillan Children's Books

This edition published 1994 by Macmillan Children's Books
a division of Macmillan Publishers Limited
25 Eccleston Place, London SW1W 9NF
Basingstoke and Oxford
www.macmillan.co.uk

Associated companies throughout the world

ISBN 0 330 33681 9

9

A CIP catalogue record for this book is available from
the British Library

Printed and bound in Great Britain by
Mackays of Chatham plc, Chatham, Kent

For Chris, Sophie and Ben

I reckon there's something wrong with me.

There must be.

Normal people don't do what I've just done—
spoil a wonderful evening and upset half the town
and ruin a perfectly good Jelly Custard Surprise.

Perhaps the heat's affected my brain.

Perhaps I've caught some mysterious disease that
makes things slip out of my hands.

Perhaps I'm in the power of creatures from
another planet who own a lot of dry-cleaning shops.

All I know is ten minutes ago my life was totally
and completely happy.

Now here I am, standing in the principal's office,
covered in raspberry jelly and lemon custard, waiting
to be yelled at and probably expelled and maybe
even arrested.

I reckon it was the heat.

It was incredibly hot in that school hall with
so many people dancing and talking in loud voices
and reaching across each other for the party pies.

And I was running around nonstop, keeping an

1

eye on the ice supply and mopping up spilt drinks and helping Amanda put out the desserts and reminding Dad to play a few waltz records in between the country stuff.

I had to sprint up onto the stage several times to stop the 'Farewell Ms Dunning' banner from drooping.

Plus, whenever I saw kids gazing at Ms Dunning and starting to look sad, I'd dash over and stick an apple fritter in their hands to cheer them up.

Every few minutes I went and stood in front of the big fan that Vic from the hardware store had lent for the night, but I still felt like the Murray–Darling river system had decided to give South Australia a miss and run down my back instead.

Amanda was great.

How a person with hair that thick and curly can stay cool on a night like this beats me.

Every time she saw me in front of the fan she gave me a grin.

Don't worry, the grin said, everything's under control and Ms Dunning's having a top time.

That's the great thing about a best friend, half the time you don't even need words.

I'd just given fresh party pies to the principal and the mayor and was heading over to the food table with the bowl of Jelly Custard Surprise when the formalities started. The music stopped and we were all deafened by the screech of a microphone being switched on and the rumble of Amanda's dad clearing his throat.

Amanda's grin vanished.

I gave her a look. Don't panic, it said, once you get up to the microphone you'll be fine.

I didn't know if it was true, but I could see it made her feel better.

'Ladies and gentlemen,' said Mr Cosgrove, 'on behalf of the Parents and Teachers Association Social Committee, it's time for the presentation to our guest of honour.'

There was a silence while everyone looked around for Ms Dunning.

She was at the food table, looking startled, gripping Darryn Peck's wrist.

I felt really proud of her at that moment.

There she was, eight and a half months pregnant, hot and weary after spending the whole afternoon making the Jelly Custard Surprise, and she was still taking the trouble to stop Darryn Peck using my apple fritters as frisbees.

No wonder we all think she's the best teacher we've ever had.

Ms Dunning let go of Darryn Peck and went over and stood next to Mr Cosgrove while he made a long speech about how dedicated she is and how sad we all are that she's leaving the school but how we all understand that babies are the future of Australia.

Then Mr Cosgrove called Amanda to the microphone.

She was so nervous she almost slipped over in a drink puddle, but once she was there she did a

3

great job. She read the speech we'd written in her loudest voice without a single mistake, not even during the difficult bit about Ms Dunning being an angel who shone with such radiance in the classroom we hardly ever needed the fluoros on.

After Amanda finished reading she presented Ms Dunning with a carved wooden salad bowl and matching carved wooden fork and spoon which the Social Committee had bought after ignoring my suggestion of a tractor.

Everyone clapped except me because I had my hands full, but I wobbled the Jelly Custard Surprise to show that I would have if I could.

Ms Dunning grinned and blushed and made a speech about how much fun she'd had teaching us and how nobody should feel sad because she'd see everyone most days when she dropped me off at school.

Even though it was a short speech, she was looking pretty exhausted by the time she'd finished.

'I'm pooped,' she grinned. 'Where's that husband of mine?'

Dad stepped forward and kissed her and she leant on his shoulder and there was more applause.

Dad gave such a big grin I thought his ears were going to flip his cowboy hat off.

I was grinning myself.

Dad's had a hard life, what with Mum dying and stuff, and a top person like him deserves a top person like Ms Dunning.

I reckon marrying Ms Dunning is the best thing

he ever did, and that includes buying the apple-polishing machine.

Seeing them standing there, smiling at each other, Ms Dunning smoothing down the fringe on Dad's shirt, I felt happier than I have all year, and I've felt pretty happy for most of it.

Which is why what happened next was so weird.

Dad cleared his throat and went down on one knee so his eyes were level with Ms Dunning's bulging tummy.

I wasn't surprised at that because he does it all the time at home. The mayor, though, was staring at Dad with his mouth open. Mayors get around a fair bit, but they probably don't often come across apple farmers who wear goanna-skin cowboy boots and sing to their wives' tummies.

As usual Dad sang a song by Carla Tamworth, his favourite country and western singer.

It was the one about the long-distance truck driver who listens to tapes of his two-month-old baby crying to keep himself awake while he's driving.

As usual Dad had a bit of trouble with a few of the notes, but nobody seemed to mind. Ms Dunning was gazing at him lovingly and everyone else was smiling and some people were tapping their feet, including the mayor.

I was enjoying it too, until Dad got to the chorus.

'Your tears are music to my ears,' sang Dad to Ms Dunning's midriff, and that's when my brain must have become heat-affected.

5

Suddenly my heart was pounding and I had a strange sick feeling in my guts.

I turned away.

And suddenly my feet were sliding and suddenly the Jelly Custard Surprise wasn't in my hands anymore.

The bowl still was, but the Jelly Custard Surprise was flying through the air.

It hit the grille of the big hardware store fan, and then everyone in the hall disappeared into a sort of sticky mist. It was just like when Dad sprays the orchard, except his mist isn't pink and it hasn't got bits of custard in it.

I stood there, stunned, while people shrieked and tried to crawl under the food table.

The mayor still had his mouth open, but now it was full of jelly.

Mr Cosgrove was staring down at his suit in horror, looking like a statue that had just been dive-bombed by a large flock of pink and yellow pigeons.

Darryn Peck was sitting in a Greek salad. I only knew it was him because of the tufts of ginger hair poking up through the sticky pink stuff that covered his face.

I blew the jelly out of my nose and ran out of the hall and thought about hiding in the stationery cupboard but came in here instead.

I'd have ended up here anyway because the principal's office is always where people are taken to be yelled at and expelled and arrested.

There's someone at the door now.

6

They seem to be having trouble opening it.

It's pretty hard getting a grip on a door handle when you've got Jelly Custard Surprise running out of your sleeves.

I'd help them if I wasn't shaking so much.

The door opened and Mr Fowler came in and it was worse than I'd imagined.

It wasn't just his sleeves that were dripping with jelly and custard, it was most of his shirt and all of his shorts and both knees.

On top of his head, in the middle of his bald patch, were several pieces of pineapple. Ms Dunning always puts crushed pineapple at the bottom of her Jelly Custard Surprise. It's delicious, but it's not really a surprise, not to us. I think it was to Mr Fowler though.

He saw me and just sort of glared at me for a bit.

I tried to stop shaking so I wouldn't drip on his carpet so much.

It was no good. I looked down and saw I was standing in a puddle of passion-fruit topping.

I made a mental note to write to the Department of Education and explain that it had dripped out of my hair and not out of Mr Fowler's lunch box.

Mr Fowler didn't seem to have noticed.

He strode over to his desk and wiped his hands on his blotter.

I waited for him to ring the District Schools Inspector and say, 'I've got a girl here who's been mute since birth and she came to us from a special school fourteen months ago and I thought she was fitting in OK but she's just sprayed two hundred people with Jelly Custard Surprise and so obviously she's not and she'll have to go back to a special school first thing in the morning'.

He didn't.

He just glared at me some more.

'I've seen some clumsy acts in this school,' he said, 'but I think you, Rowena Batts, have just topped the lot.'

I didn't reply because my hands were shaking too much to write and Mr Fowler doesn't understand sign language.

'I knew it was a mistake having food,' he continued, starting to rummage through the top drawer of his filing cabinet. 'That floor was awash with coleslaw from the word go. I nearly slipped over just before you did.'

My legs felt like they had jelly on the inside as well as the outside.

'You OK, Tonto?' said a voice from the door.

It was Dad.

His face was creased with concern and splattered with custard, and for a sec I thought he'd changed his shirt. Then I saw it was the blue satin one he'd been wearing all along, but the red jelly had turned it purple.

'I'm fine,' I said, trying to keep my hand movements small so I wouldn't flick drips onto Mr Fowler's files.

Ms Dunning came in behind Dad, just as splattered and just as concerned.

She gave me a hug.

'When you have bad luck, Ro, you really have bad luck,' she said. 'And after all the hard work you put into tonight.'

She wiped something off my left elbow, then turned to Mr Fowler.

'We want to get home and cleaned up, Frank,' she said. 'Can we talk about paying for the damage tomorrow?'

Mr Fowler looked up from the filing cabinet.

'No need,' he said, holding up a piece of paper. 'The insurance covers accidental food spillage.'

Ms Dunning gave such a big sigh of relief that a lump of pineapple slid off the top of her tummy. I caught it before it hit the carpet.

I could tell from Dad's face he wanted to get me out of there before Mr Fowler discovered a clause in the insurance policy excluding jelly.

To get to the truck we had to go through the school hall. It was full of people wiping each other with serviettes and hankies and bits torn off the 'Farewell Ms Dunning' banner.

I held my breath and hoped they wouldn't notice me.

They did.

People started glowering at me from under sticky

eyebrows and muttering things that fortunately I couldn't hear because I still had a fair bit of jelly in my ears.

Amanda came over, her hair rubbed into sticky spikes. 'If Mr Fowler tries to murder you,' she said with her hands, 'tell him to speak to me. I saw you slip.'

I felt really proud of her. Not only is she kind and loyal, but I only taught her the sign for 'murder' last week.

'Don't feel bad, Ro,' called out Megan O'Donnell's mum, scraping custard off her T-shirt with a knife. 'I'm on a diet so I'd rather have it on the outside than on the inside.'

There are some really nice people in this town.

But I do feel bad.

I felt bad all the way home in the truck, even though Dad made me and Ms Dunning laugh by threatening to drive us round the orchard on the tractor so all the codling moths would stick to us.

I feel bad now, even though I'm standing under a cool shower.

Because I didn't slip on some coleslaw and accidentally lose control of the Jelly Custard Surprise.

I threw it on purpose.

The great thing about talking in your head is you can say anything you want.

Even things you're scared to say in real life.

Even to your own Dad.

He's just been in to say goodnight.

The moment he stepped into the room I could tell he wanted to have a serious talk because he'd changed into his black shirt, the one with the yellow horseshoes on the front. Dad always wears that when he's planning a serious conversation.

'Feeling better?' he asked with his mouth.

Dad doesn't seem to talk so much with his hands these days.

'A bit better,' I said. 'How are the boots?'

'Gave them a rinse and they're good as new,' he said.

'Belt buckle?' I asked.

'Pretty yukky,' he said, grinning. 'Jelly in the eyeholes. Had to scrub it with my toothbrush.'

For about the millionth time in my life I thought how lucky I am to have a dad like him. I bet there aren't many dads who stay calm when they've got jelly in the eyeholes of their cow-skull belt buckle.

Dad cleared his throat, which meant he was either about to get musical or serious.

'Tonto,' he said, 'Amanda told me how that pud got airborne tonight. She said it was cause you turned away real quick while I was singing. I didn't think you got embarrassed any more at me having a warble in public.'

'I don't,' I said.

It's true. I did when we first came here, before people got to know Dad, because I was worried they'd think he was mental. But then one day I realised I didn't mind any more. It was at the wedding. The wedding was the happiest day of my life, and even Dad singing 'Chalk Up My Love In The Classroom Of Your Heart' to Ms Dunning at the altar didn't change that.

'So,' Dad went on, 'tonight's little mishap wasn't on account of me singing?'

I shook my head.

I know it wasn't, because Dad's sung heaps of other times since the wedding—at Ms Dunning's birthday party and at the school fund-raising bingo night and at the dawn service on Anzac Day—and no food's ended up in any electrical appliances on any of those occasions.

Dad looked relieved. Then he frowned, like he does when we're playing Trivial Pursuit and he gets a question about astronomy.

'Do you reckon there's a possibility,' he said,

'that tonight's mishap was the result of stress?'

'What stress?' I asked.

'The stress,' he said, 'of you having a teacher who's also your mum.'

'Definitely not,' I said, almost poking his eye out with my elbow. My hand movements get a bit wild when I'm being emphatic.

There's no way that could be it. I love having Ms Dunning living with us and she was tops in class. The number of times she must have been tempted to tell me to pay attention or I wouldn't get any tea, and she didn't do it once.

'The only stress I've suffered this year,' I said to Dad, 'was when that committee in Sydney ignored my nomination of her as Australian Of The Year.'

I was ropeable. How many nominations do they get that have been signed by thirty people? Even Darryn Peck signed after I gave him two dollars.

Dad looked relieved again. 'Just checking,' he said. 'By the way, Tonto, now she's not your teacher any more, it'd be real good if you could call her Claire.'

'OK,' I said, 'I'll try to remember.'

Dad frowned again, but this time really hard, like when the Trivial Pursuit question's about the digestive system of the West Australian bog leech.

I waited for him to speak.

I could see there was something else he wanted to ask me, but he was having trouble getting it out.

I decided to step in before he risked his health by standing on his head or doing any of the other things he does when there's a bit of tension in the air.

'Dad,' I said, 'I'm really happy you married Ms Dunning. I mean Claire. I think she's great and I wouldn't swap her for a prawn sandwich, not even with the crusts cut off.'

Dad grinned and gave me a big hug.

His hair smelt faintly of raspberry jelly.

'We'll have to get you some new shoes,' he said. 'Something with decent soles that'll grip coleslaw.'

I didn't say anything, I just tried to look as sleepy as I could.

Ms Dunning came in and gave me a kiss on the cheek and when I peeked she and Dad were creeping out of the room with their arms round each other.

They stopped in the hallway and kissed.

I bet there aren't many couples who still do that after a year of marriage.

It gave me a warm feeling inside.

But that was ages ago, and now I don't feel warm inside or sleepy.

I may never sleep again.

It's pretty hard to nod off when you've just chucked a dessert across a school hall and you haven't got a clue why.

Dad always reckons if you've got a problem, don't just mope around, do something about it.

When I woke up this morning I decided to do something about mine.

I grabbed my pen and tore a page off my drawing pad.

At the top in big letters I wrote, 'TO WHOM IT MAY CONCERN'.

Under it I wrote, 'SORRY'.

Then I had a think.

I wanted to choose my words carefully because you don't just scribble any old stuff when you're apologising to two hundred people.

It wasn't easy to concentrate, what with Dad revving the tractor outside and Ms Dunning whistling really loudly to herself in the kitchen, but after a bit I decided on the right words.

'If the school insurance doesn't cough up enough,' I wrote, 'send the extra dry-cleaning bills to me and I'll fix you up. It might take a while cause I only get $2.50 pocket money, but I earn extra helping

Dad in the orchard. Sorry for the inconvenience, yours faithfully, Rowena Batts. PS If there's anything that won't come out, bring the clothes round to our place. Dad knows how to shift problem stains using liquid fertiliser.'

When I'd finished I went into the kitchen to ask Ms Dunning to check the spelling.

She was standing at the stove reading the paper.

'Look at this,' she said excitedly. 'Carla Tamworth's singing at the showground, next Saturday.'

'I know,' I said.

'Dad'll be over the moon,' she said.

'That's right,' I said.

I didn't remind her that Dad and me had already been over the moon two weeks ago when the ad first appeared in the paper.

People who are having a baby in eight days go a bit vague, it's a known fact. No point making her feel embarrassed.

I made Ms Dunning take the weight off her feet while she checked my spelling and I did the eggs.

I've told her a million times that when you're having eggs with apple fritters the eggs should be runny, but she just can't seem to grasp the idea. She probably will when she's had the baby and her head clears, but.

Ms Dunning finished reading my public notice and got up and came over and put her hand on my shoulder.

'Inconvenience doesn't have an "s",' she said quietly. 'Ro, it's a good notice, but you don't have

17

to do this, you know.'

I turned the heat down under the eggs and explained to her that in small country towns if you spray jelly onto people's clothes, bitter feuds can erupt and fester for generations.

She thought about that.

Even brilliant teachers don't know everything, specially when they're originally from the city like Ms Dunning.

'If I don't make amends now,' I told her, 'in fifty years time you could find someone's parked you in at the supermarket just on the day you're rushing to get over to the bank to pick up your pension.'

Ms Dunning thought about that too, frowning.

For a sec I thought she hadn't understood all my hand movements, but then she grinned and I could see she had. She's very good at reading sign now, just not so good at speaking it.

'OK, Ro,' she said, 'go for it.'

She gave my shoulder a squeeze and hurried off to have a wee, which is something else that happens a lot when you're having a baby in just over a week.

I'll be going for it as soon as I've finished breakfast.

Actually I'm not feeling very hungry, even though the eggs are perfect.

Every time I swallow there's a knot in my guts the size of Ayers Rock.

I think I'm a bit nervous about facing everyone after last night.

I'll be OK, though, as long as I can get the notice photocopied and stuck up everywhere before an angry mob grabs me and strings me up by my feet from the Tidy Town sign.

As I left our place I saw something that made me feel better.

A rainbow sparkling from one side of the orchard to the other.

We get them sometimes when Dad's spraying the trees with the big blower and the sunlight slants through the clouds of spray.

Today's was a beauty and I decided it was a good sign.

It wasn't.

It didn't even have a pot of gold at the end of it.

Just Darryn Peck.

Halfway into town I turned a corner and there he was, coming towards me with two of his mates.

He was carrying something in a cage. At first it looked like a white feather duster with a blob of custard on it, but I knew that couldn't be right. Even Darryn Peck wouldn't carry a feather duster around in a cage.

As he got closer I saw it was a cockatoo with

a row of yellow feathers sticking out the top of its head.

Then Darryn stopped kicking dust at his mates and saw me.

His red lips stretched into a smirk.

'Oh no, it's Batts!' he shrieked, backing away pretending to be scared. 'Don't go too close, she might be carrying a trifle and slip over.'

His mates thought this was so hilarious I looked away in case they split their daks.

Then Darryn did a strange thing.

He came over to me and spoke in a quiet, serious voice, just like a normal person. 'Was that an accident last night,' he asked, 'or did you chuck that trifle on purpose?'

I was so stunned, partly by the question and partly because I'd never heard Darryn say anything in a serious voice before, that my hands stayed where they were, gripped around my rolled-up notice.

We looked at each other for a moment, then Darryn nodded slowly. 'Good one,' he said, and winked.

People generally don't like being winked at by Darryn Peck. I've seen teachers fly into a rage and send him out to stand on the oval. But as I turned away and walked on, heart thumping, Darryn and his mates chortling behind me about how funny Mr Fowler had looked with pineapple on his head, I realised I was feeling better than I had all morning.

I almost went back and told Darryn about Mr Fowler wiping his hands on his blotter, but I resisted the temptation and hurried on into town.

It was just as well I did, because when I arrived at the newsagents my name was already mud.

Two elderly women I didn't even know glared at me across the top of their wedding magazines and muttered things to each other.

When I'd finished the photocopying, I gave them a notice each and hurried out.

The main street's always busy on a Saturday morning, but today there were even more people than usual. I crept along sticking notices on power poles and rubbish bins and hoped they hadn't come to get their hands on me.

A lot of them seemed to be staring at me. I kept my eyes on the ground except when I had to reach up with the sticky tape.

Which is why I didn't see the queue until I almost walked into it.

The queue that stretched out of the dry-cleaners and along the front of the cake shop next door.

I looked down again and hoped desperately that Mr Shapiro the dry-cleaner had started selling concert tickets to make ends meet, and that the people were queueing to buy tickets for next weekend's Carla Tamworth concert.

Then I remembered that the concert is part of the Agricultural Show, so it's free.

I looked up and saw that every person in the queue was holding a dress or a suit or a skirt and blouse, each one streaked and spotted with jelly and custard stains.

I hoped Mr Shapiro's dry-cleaning machines were in good running order.

People in the queue were starting to look at me and mutter to each other.

I could feel my face going red and the knot in my guts growing back to the size of Ayers Rock including the car park and the kiosk.

I'd have given anything at that moment to be able to speak with my mouth.

Money.

Jewels.

My softball bat and the blue satin dress Dad bought me to wear at the wedding.

Anything.

Just for two minutes so I could read my apology out in a loud clear voice and everyone could see that I meant it.

I squeezed the thought out of my head and took a deep breath and walked along the queue to where I am now, in front of Mr Shapiro's window, sticking up a notice.

It's taking me ages because my heart is pounding so hard I can hardly get the sticky tape off the roll.

I'm trying to ignore everyone behind me.

I'm having this talk in my head to try and take my mind off them.

It's no good, I can feel their stares boring into the back of my neck like enraged codling moths.

People in our town hate queueing at the best of times.

I'm terrified someone'll start shouting or jostling.

I reckon that's all it'll take to turn that queue into a furious, surging mob that'll grab me and rub my nose in all those stains and cover me with custard and chook feathers and parade me round town in the back of a ute.

Oh no.

Someone's started shouting.

I braced myself against Mr Shapiro's window, hoping desperately that there were lots of officers on duty in the police station, and that they weren't watching the cricket with the sound turned up.

Then I realised it was Amanda doing the shouting.

She was calling to me from the doorway of her dad's menswear shop across the street.

'Ro,' she yelled, 'over here.'

I sprinted across the road and into the shop and crouched trembling behind a rack of trousers, hoping the people in the queue wouldn't follow. Or that if they did, they'd see all the neat piles of shirts and socks in Mr Cosgrove's shop and decide that having a riot would mean too much tidying up afterwards.

'Sorry to yell like that,' said Amanda. 'I'm serving, so I can't leave the shop.'

Then she noticed I was shaking like the mudguard on a tractor.

'What's wrong?' she asked, concerned. My hands were trembling too much to say anything so I just gave her one of the notices.

While she read it I glanced around the shop. There was only one customer and he seemed to be too busy looking at jackets to form a mob.

Mr Cosgrove was busy too, straightening each jacket on the rack after the customer had touched it.

I took some deep breaths and tried to calm down.

Mr Cosgrove turned with a smile.

'Can I help you?' he asked.

Then he saw it was me and his smile vanished.

He hurried over and steered me away from the rack of trousers.

I tried to show him that it was OK, I wasn't carrying any desserts, trifles or squishy cakes, but he wasn't paying attention.

He was glaring at Amanda.

'Outside,' he muttered to her, gesturing at me.

'Dad,' said Amanda indignantly, 'Ro's my friend.'

Amanda's getting really good at standing up to her father.

I was still feeling wobbly, so I leant against a colonial table with some polished horseshoes and a pile of neatly-folded shirts on it.

Mr Cosgrove snatched the shirts away.

'Dad,' said Amanda, even more indignant, 'last night was an accident. D'you think Ro threw that jelly on purpose?'

She gave me an apologetic grin.

I didn't want to say anything, but my hands wouldn't stay still. They've always told Amanda the

26

truth and they weren't going to stop today.

'I did throw it on purpose,' I said.

Amanda stared at my hands, so I said it again.

She looked stunned.

But only for a moment.

She probably didn't mean to do it, but she glanced around the shop at all the neat new clothes. Then she grabbed my arm and dragged me out of the shop and into the milk bar next door.

I didn't blame her.

Even best friends can't put their dad's stock at risk in a recession.

She ordered us both milkshakes, and by the time she'd asked why I'd done it and I'd told her I didn't know and she'd screwed up her face and thought about that, they were ready.

The tables were all full, but as we went over everyone stared nervously at the double strawberry malted in my hand and suddenly there was a clatter of chairs and an empty table in front of us.

We sat down.

The people at the next table shifted too.

I gave them one of my notices as they went.

The people at the other tables watched me out of the corner of their eyes and muttered to each other.

We slurped for a while and I wondered gloomily if it'll take me as long to get used to the sound of muttering as it takes people who live near the railway to get used to the sound of trains.

Then Amanda's face lit up.

'The dribble,' she said with her hands.

I stared at her blankly.

'Last night,' she continued. 'You were upset about the dribble.'

I didn't want to hurt her feelings, so I chose my words carefully. I told her it was really thoughtful of her to use her hands so the other people in the milkbar couldn't eavesdrop, but that unfortunately I didn't know what she was talking about either.

She shook her curls, cross with herself, and tried again.

'The speech,' she said. 'You were upset about the speech.'

Even before her hands stopped moving I knew that was it.

Last night, before the party, the Social Committee changed their minds about me reading our speech to Ms Dunning. They reckoned if I read it with my hands and Amanda repeated it by mouth it'd take too long.

I was really hurt and disappointed, but I had an apple fritter and got over it.

As least, I thought I did.

Obviously deep inside I didn't.

Deep inside I must have wanted to push the whole Social Committee into an apple-polishing machine, but because an apple-polishing machine was too heavy to take to the party, I chucked the Jelly Custard Surprise into the fan instead.

It's scary, but at least now I know, which is a big relief.

'You're right,' I said to Amanda. 'That's it. Thanks.'

'It must be pretty frustrating sometimes, having bits missing from your throat,' said Amanda.

I nodded.

I wanted to hug her, but she was still slurping and I knew that if I made another mess my name would be mud in this town for centuries.

I should have guessed Amanda would come up with the answer. She's an expert at working out why people do things. When I'd nominated Ms Dunning as Australian Of The Year, Amanda had twigged straight off. 'It's to put her at her ease, isn't it,' she'd said. 'Show her you don't mind her marrying your dad.' Amazing. I hadn't even given her a hint.

And now, even more amazingly, she'd worked out something I didn't even know myself.

I gave her a grateful grin and we sat there slurping. Until an awful thought hit me.

'I've been frustrated heaps of times,' I said to Amanda, 'but I've never chucked a dessert before.'

We looked at each other and I could tell from her face that she was thinking what I was thinking.

What if something's snapped in my brain?

What if I could chuck something at any time?

Without knowing in advance?

I'll never dare do the eggs again.

Or carry out a chemistry experiment in class.

Or handle nonwashable paint.

My life will be a disaster.

I could be sent back to a special school.

Suddenly I knew what I had to do.

Amanda agreed.

We said oo-roo and I hit the road.

I've never walked home from town so fast, but you can't hang about when you're in desperate need of help and there's only one person who can give it to you.

The person who was told last year that if he didn't start controlling himself and staying out of fights he'd be in deep poo and who's managed it so well this year that he hasn't had a single major outburst apart from putting peanut butter in Trent Webster's ears which doesn't count because Trent provoked him.

I can hardly believe I'm doing this.

Asking Darryn Peck for help.

I knew exactly where to find him.

In the creek at the back of our orchard.

He always goes there with his mates and I knew that's where he was heading when I bumped into him this morning.

On the way I rehearsed what I'd say.

'Darryn,' I imagined writing on my notepad, 'you're a pretty unstable person but you've stayed out of trouble pretty well this year. Any tips?'

I imagined his sneer.

'Why don't you ask your old man,' I imagined him saying. 'He's more unstable than me and he hasn't been in a single fight or embarrassing incident for ages. Earbash him.'

'Don't be a thicko,' I imagined myself writing with a patient smile, 'Dad's stable cause he married Ms Dunning. I'm too young to marry a teacher. I need to know how you do it. Come on, Darryn. You can borrow my softball bat.'

As I got to the creek I decided that last bit sounded too desperate so I mentally rubbed it out.

Darryn wasn't there.

I hunted all through the bush on both sides of the creek in case he was being a comedian and hiding, but he wasn't.

Then it hit me.

He must have gone home while I was in town.

I needed a drink before I set off on the long walk to Darryn's place, and there was no way I was drinking from the creek, not after it had been touching Darryn Peck's rude bits, so I took the track that runs round the edge of the orchard and ends up at our place.

Just as well I did, because halfway along it I heard Darryn's voice, shouting something angry that I couldn't make out.

I turned a corner and there were Darryn and his two mates, standing at the base of a big tree, chucking apples up at one of the top branches.

'Don't just sit there, dummy,' Darryn yelled at something on the branch, and hurled another apple. His face was almost as red as his lips, and his voice had gone squeaky.

'Dork-brain,' one of his mates yelled up at the tree.

Then they just grunted for a bit while they concentrated on throwing apples.

I went closer to see what they were aiming at.

It was the cockatoo.

It was just sitting on the branch, not moving, with apples crashing into the leaves around it.

I couldn't understand why it didn't dive down

and rip a beakful of hair out of Darryn Peck's head. That's what I'd have done. Or at least fly away to safety.

Then I realised the poor thing must be in shock. Little wonder.

One minute you're out for a Saturday morning walk with your owner, next minute he's having a major outburst, his first of the year, and he's chucking apples at you.

So much for Darryn Peck the self-control expert. The cockatoo looked terrified.

I wanted to scream at Darryn and his mates to pack it in, but of course I can only do that sort of thing in my head, so I ran over to Darryn and knocked the apple he was about to throw out of his hand.

He spun round, startled.

I glared at him.

His red lips went into smirk position.

'Batts,' he said. 'Oooh, I'm scared. Don't hit me with a jelly, Batts.'

I thought for a sec of hitting him with a large rock, but then I remembered the terrified bird.

I gave Darryn a look which told him to go and boil his head in a pressure cooker full of root weevils.

He didn't seem to get the message.

'Mind your own business,' he sneered. 'That cocky's my property and I'll do what I like with it.'

'He's had it for six years,' said one of his mates.

'That's right,' said Darryn and threw another apple at the cockatoo.

I pointed to the broken apples all around us on the ground.

'Those are my property,' I said, speaking on behalf of the Batts family.

Darryn stared at me blankly.

I remembered he didn't understand sign.

I pulled out my notepad.

I've learned that notes work best when they're short.

'Apple theft,' I wrote. 'Five years jail.'

It's not true, of course, but I could see it got him worried.

We stared at each other for a while.

His elephant's-bum mouth started quivering at one corner, just a bit.

Then he turned and stalked off down the road.

His mates hurried after him.

'You leaving the cocky with her?' one of them asked.

'She can keep it,' Darryn said, looking back at me. 'They should get on well together. They're both spazzos.'

I ignored that.

I had more important things to think about.

I started climbing the tree.

It took me ages to get up there, partly because Dad's taught me never to rush at a tree, and partly because I'm scared of heights.

As I edged along the branch, my heart was pounding so loudly I was worried the cockatoo would take fright and do something silly.

It didn't look as though it was up to much flying. It looked as though the most it could probably manage would be a plummet to the ground.

I tried to calm it by explaining with gentle hand movements that not all humans are like Darryn Peck, only the ones who got too close to Mrs Peck's vacuum cleaner when they were babies and had their brains sucked out through their ears.

OK, it wasn't true, and the cocky probably couldn't understand sign language anyway, but it still seemed to make it perk up a bit.

Its crest feathers, which had been lying flat on its head in a sort of cowlick, suddenly sprang up like a bright yellow mohawk hairdo.

When I'd stopped being startled and almost falling out of the tree, I leant forward and unhooked its claws from the bark as gently as I could and lifted it towards me.

Its feathers felt stiff, which I assumed was nervous tension, and I could see its dark little tongue darting around inside its beak, probably because its mouth was dry with worry.

It seemed pretty dazed, probably from seeing all those apples being wasted, and it didn't flap its wings, which was just as well for both of us.

I put it inside my shirt and climbed down, praying that it was feeling too crook to sink its beak into my flesh.

It must have been.

As I hurried towards the house, I racked my brains for anything I'd ever read or heard about helping cockatoos recover from a traumatic experience.

Nothing sprang to mind.

I could feel the cocky quivering inside my shirt.

I didn't blame it.

Living with Darryn Peck for six years would be enough to give anyone a nervous condition.

When people are in shock they're given a cup of tea, so when we got home I gave the cocky one.

It wasn't interested, so I gave it a glass of water.

It drank some of that, then tried to eat the glass.

Obviously it was hungry.

There was a note on the kitchen table saying that Dad and Ms Dunning had gone shopping, so I had to take a punt myself as to what cockies like to eat.

It wasn't a very good punt.

The cocky ignored the corned beef, sniffed the cheese, spat out the Coco-Pops and did a poo on the apple fritter.

Then it closed its eyes.

I realised the poor thing must be exhausted.

I grabbed an apple box and made a bed in it with some towels from the bathroom and carefully laid the cocky inside.

That wasn't such a good move either.

I could tell the cocky wasn't comfortable by the way it scrabbled its claws and looked at me unhappily with its dark eyes and did a wee on my towel.

I remembered that some birds like to sleep on a perch.

It was worth a try.

I took all the clothes on hangers out of my wardrobe and pulled the top shelf out to make some headroom and lifted the cocky onto the hanging rail.

No sooner had it gripped the wood with its claws than its eyes closed and its head dropped and I was sure I could hear faint snoring.

It's been like that for hours.

I've been sitting here on my bed watching it in case it has a nightmare about apples.

I've also been working out how I'm going to break it to Dad and Ms Dunning that we've got a new addition to the family.

Sometimes good luck comes along exactly when you need it.

Like this arvo.

Dad and Ms Dunning came back with heaps of shopping, not just supermarket stuff but loads of parcels and boxes too.

While I was helping them carry it all in from the truck, I saw them looking at each other sort of sheepishly.

'Um, Tonto old mate,' said Dad, 'we haven't actually got anything for you.'

It was perfect.

There's nothing like parents feeling a bit sheepish to help things along when you're asking if you can have a cockatoo.

Dad and Ms Dunning were a bit alarmed at first, probably because they thought I was talking about buying a new one and they'd just spent all their money.

But when I showed them the one dozing in my wardrobe, and explained it was an abused bird that

I'd rescued from a dangerously unstable kid, they relaxed.

I told them that if the cocky could live with us I'd feed it and care for it and teach it to use the bathroom.

'Please, please, please, please, please,' I said until my hands ached.

I saw from Dad's face that he wanted to have a serious talk. Not with me, with Ms Dunning. I almost went and got his black shirt with the horseshoes but decided not to.

I stayed in here on my bed while Dad and Ms Dunning went into the kitchen.

I crossed my fingers so tightly they went numb.

After what seemed like ages, Dad and Ms Dunning came back in. They had their arms round each other, which I knew was a good sign.

'Well Tonto,' said Dad, 'if you promise to feed it and clean it, you can keep it. I'll build it a cage in the packing shed.'

I gave them both a huge hug.

'There's one more condition,' added Dad. 'Darryn Peck's got to agree you can have it.'

I told them I was sure Darryn would agree because it's doing him a favour too.

This way he won't ever get into trouble with the law for mistreating a bird and possibly end up in a bloody shoot-out with officers from the RSPCA.

Ms Dunning held out a big shiny red apple.

'It'll probably be hungry when it wakes up,' she said.

I was really moved because it was exactly the same as the one I gave her the day she moved in with us.

Watching the cocky happily snoozing away I can see it's already feeling like one of the family.

Judging by the snores, though, I don't think it'll be waking up till the morning.

A big sleep's probably just what the poor thing needs.

In the morning I'll cut its apple up and we can have breakfast together on the verandah.

I'm feeling really attached to it already.

Almost like a parent.

Which is fine with me because in my experience parents hardly ever snap and even when they do they hardly ever chuck desserts, eggs, chemicals or nonwashable paint.

I knew something was wrong as soon as I woke up.

Dad was shouting.

Ms Dunning was yelling.

I could smell fish frying and nobody at our place likes fried fish.

I jumped out of bed and hurried towards the kitchen.

Something stabbed me in the feet.

I looked down and saw that my carpet was covered with lumps of apple and splinters of wood.

My floor looked like Tasmania, the bit that's been woodchipped.

The kitchen looked worse.

Apart from the woodchips all over the floor and the table and the sink, it was full of smoke.

Dad and Ms Dunning were standing on chairs holding brooms. Dad was shouting at Ms Dunning to get down because she shouldn't be climbing on chairs in her condition, and Ms Dunning was ignoring him and poking her broom up the chimney.

41

A cloud of soot floated down into her face, followed by a white feather.

My heart was thumping.

'Get down here, dork-brain,' Ms Dunning yelled up the chimney, 'or you're dead meat.'

I was shocked.

That's no way to talk to a cockatoo with a nervous condition.

I reminded myself that it wasn't Ms Dunning's fault, she's just been spending too much time with Darryn Peck and his mates.

Then I squeezed myself into the fireplace and climbed up onto the big log we keep there in summer and lifted both my hands up into the blackness.

I touched feathers.

I wondered if a cockatoo can recognise friendly hands in pitch darkness when it's got other things on its mind, like being called a dork-brain.

My fingers all stayed connected to my hands, so obviously it can.

Gently I lifted the cocky down.

In the darkness I could see a gleaming eye watching me.

As I wriggled out of the fireplace with the cocky clasped to my chest, Dad and Ms Dunning advanced towards me.

Their eyes were gleaming too.

'That bird's a flaming menace,' said Dad. He said it with his mouth, partly because he always speaks with his mouth when he's angry, and partly because his hands were full of bits of splintered wood.

'Look what it did to Claire's hand-carved salad bowl.'

I glanced down at the cocky's curved black beak. It looked strong, but not that strong.

'And the vicious cheese-brain had a go at my buckle,' continued Dad.

I looked at his belt and suddenly I felt the cocky's head feathers tickling me under the chin. I wasn't sure if that was because it had just gone mohawk or because my mouth had just fallen open.

The metal buckle looked as if it had been attacked with pliers. The Harley Davidson had a bent wheel and the skeleton riding it was completely missing a ribcage.

I looked at the cocky's beak again. Perhaps its mother had swallowed a lump of tungsten steel thinking it was a gumnut.

'And,' said Ms Dunning, 'it had a go at the kitchen table and the dresser and snatched the washing-up sponge out of my hand and nearly caused a fire.'

She pointed to the sink, where a charred sponge was floating in the frying pan.

It hadn't been fish after all.

'Just give me a few moments alone with it,' I said.

Dad and Ms Dunning looked confused. Perhaps they thought I meant the sponge. It's not easy expressing yourself clearly when you've got your hands full of sooty cockatoo.

I retreated into my room and put the cocky onto what was left of the hanging rail.

We both looked at the large jagged hole in the side of my wardrobe.

'It's OK,' I said, moving my hands slowly. 'Don't feel bad. You just panicked. That's normal, waking up in a strange place.'

I could tell from its blank expression and the big poo it did on my best shoes that it didn't have a clue what I was saying.

I wrote it a note.

It was worth a try. Cockies are very smart. I've seen them on telly pedalling little bikes and drawing raffles.

It ate the note.

There are times when it's a real pain not being able to speak. You want to scream with frustration, except of course you can't. So you make do with what you've got.

I put my face close to the cocky's and gave it a look.

'Don't be scared, you poor little thing,' the look said. 'I want to help you.'

'Rack off,' said the cocky.

I couldn't believe it.

Then I realised I must have misheard.

I was making the cocky feel nervous by being too close, that was all, and it had asked me to back off.

I moved my face back a bit.

'Get lost, dork-brain,' said the cocky. 'You smell. Go and fall off a rock.'

I was shocked.

But I tried to be understanding.

I gave the cockatoo another look.

'Don't be cross,' my look said, 'everything's going to be fine.'

'Get stuffed,' said the cocky.

I changed the look to 'I'm your friend'.

'Go kiss a chook,' said the cocky.

My face was aching, but I had one more go.

I gave it my best 'I'm going to look after you' expression.

'Suck a turnip,' said the cocky, and bit me on the nose.

After Dad had bathed the wound and put some antiseptic cream and a band-aid on it and the pain had died down, we got a metal bucket and put the cocky inside and fixed some strong chook-wire over the top.

Dad offered to drive it to Darryn Peck's, but I said I'd take it by foot. I could tell Dad was itching to get at Ms Dunning's salad bowl with the glue.

We're almost there, which is a relief.

It's not much fun walking with a bird in a bucket who keeps telling you to bite your bum.

It's a real shame because if it had a different personality we could have been really close.

As it is I'll be pleased to see the back of it.

The last thing I want in my life at the moment is an angry cockatoo.

There's a Carla Tamworth song called 'Compost Heap In My Heart' about a keen gardener whose sweetheart leaves her for a stock and station agent. Totally and completely grief-stricken, she goes out into the back yard and starts pulling his old cabbage stalks out of the compost heap. It's all she's got left of him. Then, deep in the compost, she finds a hose nozzle and remembers she hasn't washed the car for weeks.

That happened to me today.

I don't mean I found a hose nozzle in a compost heap.

I mean I started out doing one thing and ended up doing something else.

I started out taking a cocky with crook manners back to Darryn Peck and ended up nearly committing murder.

And now I feel sick in the guts.

Perhaps I'll feel better if I stop thinking about it.

That's what the keen gardener does. She stops

thinking about her sweetheart and concentrates on cleaning the car and feels much better. Specially when her sweetheart comes round to get his hose nozzle and slips on the wet driveway and breaks his pelvis.

Darryn Peck deserves to break his pelvis.

Well, get a cramp in it anyway.

The way he's treated this cocky is a disgrace.

Six years they've been together and when I arrived at his place he wouldn't even say hello to it.

'I don't want it,' he said. 'It's yours. It was a fair swap. I don't care if the apples weren't ripe.'

I could tell the cocky was hurt. When Darryn opened the front door it had put its crest feathers into the mohawk position so they stuck up through the mesh over the bucket. Now it slowly slid them back into the cowlick position.

I got out my notebook and pointed out to Darryn that a cockatoo is a living creature with feelings, even if it does have a violent nature and a mouth like a sewer pipe.

Darryn stared at the note, confused.

'What,' he said, 'you mean it's got bad breath?'

I wrote Darryn another note mentioning some of the things the cocky had been doing and saying.

He read it and I could tell he was genuinely surprised because his eyes went big and round, and Darryn's one of those people who thinks it's cooler to keep your eyes half closed all the time.

'Don't lie,' he said. 'Sticky Beak can't talk.

47

Sticky's never said a word, not even when I ran the electric current from the front door bell through his feet. He's a brainless dummy.'

The cocky looked up at him with moist eyes.

I took a deep breath and scribbled furiously on my pad.

'Perhaps if you weren't so cruel,' I wrote, 'he'd want to talk to you.'

'Bull,' said Darryn. 'Sticky's a dummy and a no-hoper. I've got a much better pet now. That's why I was setting feather-brain here free yesterday. Till you stuck your nose in.'

Darryn was lucky there wasn't a Jelly Custard Surprise nearby.

I stared at him in disgust.

No wonder Sticky Beak was so upset this morning.

This loyal loving pet had been dumped in the bush just because his fickle selfish owner had got some flashy buzzard or eagle or something.

Darryn must have seen my disgust because he started making excuses.

'I was returning him to his natural whatdyacallit,' said Darryn, 'habitat. Giving him his freedom. And if you think you can dump him back on me you can go fall off a rock.'

I wondered what sort of a jail sentence I'd get for giving a heartless monster a whack round the head with a metal bucket. Then I remembered the bucket had a cockatoo in it who'd already suffered more than enough.

I made do with a note.

'I'm not dumping him back on you,' I wrote.

I meant it. There was no way I was going to leave Sticky Beak at the mercy of heartless Darryn The Torturer Peck.

'I just came to find out what he eats,' I wrote. Lying doesn't count when it's to an inhuman fiend.

'Stay here,' said Darryn and went into the house.

There was an explosion of high-pitched barking and for a horrible moment I thought I was stuck with a cockatoo that ate dogs.

Then Darryn came back with a pinky-brown poodle yapping round his feet and handed me a plastic bucket full of striped seeds.

'Normally I'd charge you ten bucks for this,' he said, 'but you can have it for free if you rack off and never come back.'

I took the bucket.

Darryn picked up the poodle and I picked up Sticky Beak's bucket and walked away.

I could hear Darryn talking to the poodle, and the poodle replying in a sort of high-pitched growl.

'If you want a pet that can really talk,' Darryn shouted after me, 'get a poodle.'

That's when I started feeling sick in the guts.

I only just managed to stop myself from going back and making Darryn swallow all the birdseed. While it was still in the bucket.

I've been boiling inside ever since, and I'm nearly home.

I think that's just about the worst thing in the

whole world that one living creature can do to another.

Give it the flick just cause a replacement comes along that can talk better.

As I walked up our orchard road I tried to ignore the pain from the two buckets nearly dragging my arms off.

I had to think what to do.

I thought about telling Dad and Ms Dunning what sort of a life Sticky had had with Darryn Peck in the hope that they'd understand.

'We understand,' said Dad in my head, ruffling Sticky's crest feathers understandingly.

'We'd probably chew up salad bowls too,' said Ms Dunning in my head, 'if someone connected our feet to a front door bell.'

But what if they didn't say that?

What if they said, 'Get that vicious cheese-brain out of this house immediately'?

A bird could be killed stone dead by the shock and hurt of being rejected and abandoned twice in one weekend.

And even if Sticky survived, what if Dad took him over to the RSPCA depot with a note saying 'never to be released' and the poor thing ended up in some institution?

I knew what that'd be like.

I was in an institution for five years, and even though mine was a pretty good special school, I still spent a lot of nights crying.

I couldn't risk it.

So I didn't take Sticky Beak to see Dad and Ms Dunning, I took him to the old shed.

I reckoned it was a pretty safe alternative because Dad never uses the old shed. He reckons it's too far from the house.

Which it is if you've got to walk back from it after a hard day in the orchard, but it's not if you're looking for somewhere to hide a cockatoo with a loud voice and a sour view of the world.

The walls of the old shed are thicker than the walls of my wardrobe, but I couldn't afford to take any risks.

I had to think beak-proof.

I crept to the packing shed where Dad keeps his tools and junk and peeked inside.

Dad wasn't there.

As quietly as I could I borrowed his wire cutters and a roll of tying wire.

Behind the cool room were some sheets of metal from when the cool room was built and some rolls of thick chook wire from when the previous people kept chooks.

I had to be quiet dragging them over, but once I got them into the old shed I could make as much noise as I liked.

I've never built a cage before.

There must be some method of getting all the sides to stand exactly upright, but I couldn't crack it.

Still, I reckon what I've done'll do the trick.

I used the metal stakes Dad ties young trees to for the corners, and about a kilometre of tying wire, so it's pretty sturdy, and it's big enough for Sticky to fly around in as long as he doesn't try to get up too much speed.

And from the outside of the old shed you wouldn't even know it's there.

Sticky likes it.

Once I'd wired a branch across a corner for a perch he was onto it quicker than a little kid onto monkey bars.

I found some old metal dishes for his water and seed, and then gave him several meaningful looks.

In order they said:

'Don't be frightened.'

'We can go on outings.'

'This is just until Dad and Ms Dunning calm down about the wood chips.'

'Be good.'

Sticky went from mohawk to cowlick, so I could tell he understood.

I wired the last piece of chook wire into place and gave Sticky Beak a 'see you later' wave.

'Jump off a rock,' said Sticky, which I'm beginning to think is just his way of saying thanks.

I shut the door of the old shed and came over here to the packing shed to put the wire cutters back.

I've been standing here ever since having this conversation in my head.

I hated leaving Sticky there so I guess I'm trying to convince myself that I'm doing the right thing.

Well it's a bit late now cause I've done it.

What's that noise?

It's someone coming over from the house.

It's Dad.

Oh no, I'm still holding the wire cutters.

Too late.

He's seen me.

I'm lying here listening to a Carla Tamworth tape on my Walkman trying not to think about what's just happened.

It's not working.

The songs keep reminding me.

First there was the one about the heart that's aching so much that even two aspirin and a eucalyptus menthol oil rub can't take away the pain.

I spooled through that one.

Then there was the one about the woman who wants to cry but can't, not even when she goes to work in a sandwich bar making salad rolls with lots of onion.

I spooled through that one too.

And now, the final straw, I'm listening to one about a bloke who can't see things even when they're staring him in the face.

Not his clean socks or the crack in his bathroom mirror or his dentist who's secretly in love with him.

Me and Dad are like that bloke.

I don't mean because our dentist is secretly in love with us. The only thing our dentist Mr Webster loves is collecting rocks and that's no secret because he has the magazines in his waiting room.

I mean because me and Dad can't see things when they're staring us in the face either.

With Dad it's little things like not noticing I was holding the wire cutters when he walked into the packing shed this arvo.

'G'day Tonto,' he said, 'we've been wondering where you'd got to. There's something we'd like you to take a squiz at.'

For a horrible moment I was sure they'd found Sticky.

Ayers Rock dropped with a thud into my lower gut.

Then Dad grinned and said, 'Come on, race you back to the house', and I knew they hadn't.

He turned and started sprinting and I put the wire cutters back before starting off after him.

As I caught up to him I noticed he had blue paint in his hair.

Inside the house he made me close my eyes and then led me into the junk room.

Or what used to be the junk room.

When I opened my eyes Dad and Ms Dunning were standing there grinning like game-show hosts.

Ms Dunning had pink paint in her hair.

I could see why.

The entire room was pink.

Except for a blue ceiling and a blue light switch.

And it was full of stuff.

Not the old wellies and tractor parts and fishing rods and eskies and record players and camping gear and apple boxes that used to be there.

New stuff.

A cot decorated with sleepy bunnies and a change table with bashful koalas on it and a quilt covered with playful dolphins and curtains crawling with very friendly possums and a light shade infested with happy-go-lucky goannas.

'What do you reckon?' grinned Dad.

'We hope you approve of your new brother or sister's accommodation,' grinned Ms Dunning.

I tried to grin too, but I guess it wasn't very convincing.

Ms Dunning came over and put her arm round me.

'Ro,' she said quietly, 'we know you're disappointed about your pet, but we've got to be realistic.'

'That's right, Tonto,' said Dad gently. 'We can't have a kamikaze cocky in the same house as a bub, eh?'

'That's not what I'm disappointed about,' I replied. 'I thought the baby was going to sleep in my room.'

That had been the plan. We'd talked about it, me and Dad. It had been my idea, so that if the baby woke up in the night between feeds I could rock it back to sleep or keep it amused with hand-shadows on the wall. I can do a great shark.

'It was a really kind offer, love,' said Ms Dunning, 'but we've decided it'll be better off in the room next to us.'

'Claire's right,' said Dad. 'Better to have it where we can hear it yelling its little lungs out, eh?'

That's when it hit me.

The real reason I threw the Jelly Custard Surprise.

How come I didn't see it before?

It's been staring me in the face for months.

Well, hours, anyway, since I left Darryn Peck's.

The shock of finally seeing it made my heart go like a spray pump, and the smell of the paint started to make me feel like throwing up, so I came in here for a lie-down.

Usually if I want to blot something out of my mind the Walkman works really well.

Not tonight.

Even when I turn it up really loud and close my eyes really tight I can still see Darryn standing on his verandah holding the poodle, grinning like a loon because it can talk.

And Dad standing next to him doing exactly the same.

Except Dad isn't holding a poodle, he's holding a baby.

Dad always reckons if something's making me unhappy I should tell him about it.

He reckons it's better for a person to lay it out on the table than bottle it up and end up hiring a skywriter or something.

So first thing this morning I went out to the orchard and told him.

I was really glad I did.

At first.

'G'day Tonto,' Dad said, 'you come for a yak?'

I nodded.

I like yakking to Dad when he's on the tractor because he has to speak with his hands. Dad's got a pretty loud voice but it isn't a match for a 120-horsepower diesel.

I jumped up onto the front of the tractor so Dad could keep on slashing weeds while we talked.

'About last night,' Dad said. 'Don't worry, love, you'll get to spend heaps of time with the bub.'

'I know I will,' I said.

I took a deep breath.

My hands were shaking.

I hoped Dad would think it was the vibrations from the motor.

'I'm just worried,' I said, 'that when you've got a kid that can speak with its mouth, you won't want to spend heaps of time flapping your hands about with me.'

I tried to keep my hands relaxed while I said it. If you're not careful, when you're very tense you can get cramp in the middle of a sentence.

Dad stared at me for a long time.

The tractor started to shudder.

'Dad,' I said, 'you're slashing a tree trunk.'

He turned the tractor off, leant forward, grabbed me under the arms and swung me onto his lap.

It felt good, even though his belt buckle was stabbing me in the kidney.

'Ro,' he said quietly, 'that's dopey.'

Then he slid me onto the seat next to him and jumped up onto the engine cover and took his hat off and put one hand over his heart and tilted his head back and yelled up at the trees.

'I swear on my Grannies and Jonathans,' he shouted, 'that no kid will ever come between me and my precious Tonto, cross my heart and hope to get root weevil.'

I glowed inside.

I would have glowed even more if he'd looked at me and said it quietly, but with Dad you have to take him the way he is.

He jumped down from the engine and I slid down

from the seat and he picked me up and hugged me so tight that his belt buckle left an imprint on my tummy.

I glowed even more and Ayers Rock suddenly melted away and all that was left was a wonderful feeling that everything was going to be OK for ever and ever.

It lasted for about ten seconds.

Less time than the red back-to-front rodeo rider above my bellybutton.

Because I ruined it.

I've never known when to keep my hands quiet.

'For a moment there,' I said to Dad, 'I thought you were going to sing.'

Dad grinned.

'Almost did,' he said, 'but I couldn't think of a song that said exactly what I wanted to say.'

'Never mind,' I said, 'perhaps Carla Tamworth'll sing one at the concert on Saturday.'

Dad's face clouded.

'I've been meaning to tell you,' he said, 'I can't go to the concert on Saturday.'

I stared at him.

'Sorry Tonto,' he said. 'Not with the baby due on Sunday. Too much to do. You do understand, eh?'

I nodded.

I couldn't move my face, only my neck.

'Good on you,' said Dad. 'You can go with Amanda, eh?'

I nodded again.

'Run off and have your breakfast then, love,' he said, and fired up the tractor.

I walked away.

At that moment I couldn't have forced food down myself with a crowbar, but I knew Sticky Beak would be hungry.

When I got over here to the old shed and opened the door, Sticky blinked at me from inside his cage.

He looked as stunned as I felt.

Perhaps cockies have got super-sensitive hearing and he couldn't believe what he'd just heard.

A man who once drove six hours to get to a Carla Tamworth concert saying he can't be bothered taking his daughter to one six minutes away.

I wonder if cockies know about child neglect?

I shouldn't be talking like this, not even in my head.

Dad's just doing what any normal person would do in his position. Concentrating on the birth of his new baby. All fathers get a bit sidetracked when they've got a new kid on the way. Specially when it's one that doesn't have anything wrong with it.

What's so bad about that?

Nothing, and I shouldn't be blubbing like this, it's stupid.

I can see Sticky thinks so too.

I'm making his seed all wet.

He's just told me to fall off a rock.

I think he's trying to cheer me up.

Poor Sticky, he's the one who should be crying, not me. Stuck in here all by himself trying to recover from a nervous condition brought on by six years of inhuman treatment by a monster.

Darryn The Heartless Peck's the one who should be punished, not Dad.

I'm so excited.

All Sticky's problems are solved.

Well, they will be soon.

Once Amanda gets written permission to use her parents' video camera.

What's more, if my plan works, no Australian cockatoo or budgie or dog or cat or hampster or mouse need ever suffer again what Sticky has suffered.

Going to school this morning I didn't have a clue that this was going to be such an important day in the history of pet care.

For starters, I'd completely forgotten we've got a new teacher. I only remembered when Ms Dunning stopped the truck in front of the school gates and handed me a jar of home-made apple sauce.

'For your new teacher,' she said.

I groaned inside.

'Come on, Ro,' said Ms Dunning, 'a prezzie means a lot to us teachers on our first day.'

I couldn't believe it.

She's only been semi-retired for two days and

she's already forgotten that only crawlers and bad spellers give new teachers presents. That's why I wasn't carrying a plate of apple fritters.

I was about to remind her, but then I realised she must just be having a vague spell and I decided not to hurt her feelings. It can't be much fun, carrying a baby round inside you that uses up so much oxygen there's not enough left for your brain.

When I got out of the truck, all the kids that had crowded round to wave at Ms Dunning backed away, all nervously eyeing the jar of apple sauce in my hand.

I walked through them, hoping they'd notice the jar had a lid on and that there wasn't a single hardware store fan in the playground.

They didn't.

I could only see one kid who looked relaxed.

Darryn Peck.

He was standing just inside the school gate, smirking at me.

'Careful Battsy,' he said, 'don't trip over.'

I walked past.

He started walking behind me.

I ignored him.

I knew he was going to try and trip me, and I knew I could handle it.

I was wrong.

What threw me was that he used his brain.

He waited till I was almost across the playground, then gave a screeching cry, like a cockatoo.

For a sec I thought it was Sticky, that he'd escaped

and was looking for me.

I glanced up and that's when Darryn stuck his foot out.

I felt myself falling forward and my only thought was not to let go of the jar.

Then I realised I already had.

Me and the jar flew through the air.

I slammed into the ground.

The jar smashed through Mr Fowler's office window.

After a while, when I'd worked out which sounds were glass breaking and which were my ears ringing, someone lifted me to my feet.

It was Amanda.

She was white with fury and screaming at Darryn Peck.

'You're dead meat, Peck,' she yelled. 'My uncle's a solicitor.'

Darryn Peck was looking pretty pale too, but that was because he could see Mr Fowler storming towards us.

Mr Fowler was angrier than any of us had ever seen him.

He was so angry that not one person laughed at the apple sauce on his head.

'What happened?' he thundered.

There was chaos as everyone tried to tell him something different.

I kept out of it because my knees had started to hurt a lot and I wanted to see if there was any blood coming through my jeans.

After a few seconds Mr Fowler sent everyone to their classrooms.

Amanda hovered, still furious, still shouting, until Mr Fowler threatened to expel her.

Then he took me into his office.

The next few minutes were pretty hard on my nerves, partly because Mr Fowler wouldn't let me speak, and partly because he kept pacing up and down on his glass-covered carpet and I was worried he'd cut himself.

It was dumb. There I was, the victim of a tele-movie-sized injustice, and I was more worried about whether one of the people responsible would slash a major artery in his foot and I'd have to knot his whistle cord round his leg to stop the blood flow.

'I don't know what happened out there,' said Mr Fowler, 'and I probably never will. So I'll be charitable and assume it was an accident. That's two, Batts, in four days. One accident is unlucky. Two is careless. If there's a third . . .'

He stopped and put his face close to mine.

Apple sauce dripped onto my shoe.

'. . . if there's a third, watch out.'

He turned away and I pulled my notebook out to scribble a note asking for a lawyer and a broom to sweep up the broken glass.

Before I could start writing, there was a knock on the door and a bloke stepped into the office. He was wearing jeans and a multicoloured shirt and he had a ponytail.

Great, I thought, here am I in the middle of

a travesty of justice and some high-school kid who's off sick with brain damage wanders into the wrong school.

'This is Mr Segal,' said Mr Fowler, 'your new teacher. Take her away, Mr Segal, before I forget I'm a Rotarian.'

On the way to class Mr Segal made conversation.

I wasn't really in the mood because my knees were hurting and I wanted some time to myself to plan Darryn Peck's death, but I could see Mr Segal was trying hard so I joined in.

'So,' said Mr Segal, 'you're Rowena Batts.'

I nodded.

'Mr Fowler's told me all about you,' said Mr Segal.

I nodded again.

'Never feel inferior,' said Mr Segal.

I shook my head. I could see he meant well.

'Pictures,' said Mr Segal, 'are more important than words.'

He smiled.

I smiled.

I didn't have a clue what he was on about.

Then I realised he must have been talking about his shirt, which had pictures of fish all over it.

It wasn't till much later, in class, that I realised he was talking about television.

By that time Mr Segal had talked about television a lot. He told us he believes television isn't studied enough in schools. We clapped and whistled, partly because we agreed with him and partly because you

68

have to see how far you can go with a new teacher.

When we'd finished he told us we were going to spend the last three weeks of the school year studying television.

We clapped and whistled some more.

'Starting with a project,' he said when the noise had died down. 'Tomorrow you start making your own TV programmes.'

We stared at him in stunned silence.

For a fleeting moment I thought that perhaps he was a brain-damaged high-school kid after all.

'Hands up,' said Mr Segal, 'whose parents have got a video camera.'

Then we understood.

About half the class put their hands up.

I didn't. We can't afford a video camera. Not with an apple-polishing machine and a luxury nursery to pay for. But I was relieved to see Amanda with her hand up.

Mr Segal explained the project.

We've got to split into groups and we've got one week to make any TV programme we like as long as it's not rude or offensive to minority groups.

After the bell went, me and Amanda agreed to keep our group small.

Just her and me.

Then I saw Megan O'Donnell wandering around not in a group. I hate seeing kids left out of things just cause they're slow readers so I looked at Amanda and Amanda nodded and opened her mouth to ask Megan to join our group. Before she could, though,

Megan was grabbed by Lucy and Raylene Shapiro who asked her to help them make a documentary about the human side of dry-cleaning.

It was for the best. Megan's a nice person but she can get pretty nervous and she wouldn't have been comfortable doing what I've got in mind.

'Shall we do a comedy or a drama?' asked Amanda.

I told her I was thinking about something different and wrote it out so she'd get all the details first time.

'Let's do,' I said, 'a fearless in-depth current affairs report exposing to the world Darryn Peck's heartless and brutal treatment of poor old Sticky.'

Amanda grinned and nodded.

'Great,' she said, 'it's just what he deserves. Who's Sticky?'

Sticky's really excited too.

I've just told him about the project.

I didn't tell him last night because I didn't want him to suffer the crushing disappointment if Amanda's parents said no about the video camera.

I needn't have worried.

Amanda came running into school this morning with a bag over her shoulder and a big grin on her face.

'I've got it,' she yelled.

Darryn Peck looked up from Trent Webster's video camera which he was trying to focus on a pimple on Doug Walsh's bottom.

'Hope it's not catching,' he smirked.

He and his mates fell about.

Me and Amanda just smiled quietly to each other.

We resisted the temptation to tell him that soon he won't have much to laugh about because we didn't want him running off to South America and hiding.

As it turned out, it wouldn't have mattered, because for the whole day we didn't even get to

71

take the lens cap off the camera.

For a bloke who wears fish shirts, Mr Segal's a real stickler for paperwork.

First he insisted on seeing written permission from the parents of everyone who'd brought a camera in.

Then he wasted hours ringing up Trent Webster's parents. He thought Trent's note was forged just because 'camera' was spelt without an 'e'. If he'd asked us we could have explained that Trent's mum had to leave school when she was eleven to look after the goats.

Then Raylene Shapiro put her hand up and said that her dad was wondering if the school insurance would cover damage to his camera.

Mr Segal called Mr Fowler in and asked him.

He said he'd check.

I was adjusting Amanda's camera strap at the time, and when Mr Fowler saw me with a camera in my hand he went visibly pale.

Then, just when me and Amanda thought we could start shooting our in-depth report, Mr Segal announced that first we all had to write scripts.

We did that for the rest of the day.

It was a bit tricky because we didn't want Darryn Peck to know we were writing about him, so we used a code name.

Poodle.

Mr Segal thinks we're doing an in-depth report about dogs who are mean to cockatoos.

At least writing the script gave me something

to show Sticky when I got home. I don't think he'd ever seen a current affairs script before because he tried to eat it.

'Sticky,' I said, 'stop that. Don't you want to be a star and an object of pity who's allowed to sleep in my room again?'

I don't think he understood the hand movements because he just looked at me with his beak open.

I wished I had Amanda there to explain it to him by mouth.

Then I remembered what Mr Segal had said about pictures being more important than words. I pulled out my notepad and drew Sticky a picture of me playing the in-depth report to Dad and Ms Dunning on our video and them tearfully inviting Sticky to live with us in the house.

He stared at it for ages and I could see his eyes getting moister.

I drew him another picture, of Darryn Peck being arrested by RSPCA officers and sentenced to ten years hard labour cleaning out the dog pound.

Sticky put his head under his wing and seemed a bit upset, so I reduced Darryn's sentence to five years.

It was the third picture that got Sticky really excited. I did it on two pages, and it showed our report being broadcast on telly, and people all over Australia who were about to abandon or neglect cockatoos thinking again.

I put in a few people who were about to abandon or neglect other things as well.

Dogs and cats.

Hampsters.

Kids.

Those people were all thinking again too.

Dad was one of them.

'Bottom plops,' said Sticky.

Poor old Sticky, he finds it really hard to express his emotions.

I know that inside he was just as excited and moved as I was.

I never realised making in–depth current affairs programmes was so hard.

For starters there's focusing the camera properly and waiting for planes to fly over so they don't mess up the sound.

Then there's asking the reporter if she'd mind changing her orange and purple striped T-shirt for a blue one and taking off the green eye shadow.

And on top of all that there's waiting for Ms Dunning to go into town for her check–up and Dad to go over to slash weeds at the other side of the orchard so you can do the introduction in the old shed without being sprung.

No wonder it costs millions when the networks do it.

We didn't get started till nearly lunchtime.

'OK,' I said when the mail plane had finally disappeared and all we could hear was Dad murdering weeds in the distance, 'camera going, take one.'

Amanda stepped forward onto the spot I'd

75

marked on the floor in front of Sticky's cage.

'This poor mistreated bird,' she said in a loud clear voice, 'has suffered some of the crookest treatment you could imagine.'

'Pig's bum,' said Sticky.

Amanda collapsed into giggles.

'It's just his way of agreeing with you,' I said.

Amanda collapsed into more giggles.

Some reporters have no respect for their director.

'Camera going, take two,' I said.

'This poor neglected bird . . .' said Amanda.

'Andy's been sick in the fridge,' said Sticky.

Amanda laughed so hard she had to bite her clipboard.

I could see it wasn't going to be easy.

I calmed myself down by telling myself that every TV current affairs show has a few of these sort of problems on the first day.

An hour later I wasn't so sure.

'Take thirty-two,' I said, my hand aching.

'This poor neglected . . .' said Amanda.

'Turnip,' said Sticky.

'I can't do it,' screamed Amanda. 'Not with him interrupting. That's it. I resign.'

I sat Amanda down and got her a drink and while she was having it I showed Sticky the pictures again to remind him how important it was that he keep his beak shut.

Then I held up four fingers to remind him that Ms Dunning's having a baby in four days so we can't afford to waste time.

He stared at my fingers, tongue darting about in his beak.

I knew how he felt. Thinking about it makes my mouth go dry too.

Amanda came over and had a look at the pictures.

She spent a long time staring at the people who had planned to abandon cockies and hampsters and kids but were changing their minds.

Then she looked at me and I could see her eyes getting moister.

'Sorry,' she said. 'Let's try it again.'

I didn't say 'Take thirty-three' because I didn't want to depress her. I just started the camera and waved.

'This poor mistreated bird,' said Amanda, 'has suffered some of the crookest treatment you could imagine.' She glanced down at her clipboard like a professional. 'In tonight's programme we talk to the boy who did it and doesn't care. A boy who . . .'

That's when the battery ran out.

I put the camera down so I'd have two hands to swear with, and Amanda explained that the camera had only come with one battery, and that it takes twelve hours to recharge.

We didn't waste the afternoon though.

We spent it teaching Sticky some nice things to say to Dad and Ms Dunning when they invite him to join the family.

It was hard work, but by the end of the afternoon he could say 'G'day' and 'Pig's bottom'.

The battery should be charged in another six hours.

It would be less, but Ms Dunning's using heaps of electricity in the kitchen. She's had the food processor going all evening, making a lemon and lime Jelly Custard Surprise for the Cake And Pudding section in the Agricultural Show on Saturday.

I hope she wins because then she and Dad will be in the right frame of mind to watch a moving and thought-provoking in-depth current affairs report.

OK, I admit it, filming Sticky up the tree was my idea, but if we hadn't tried it we'd never have seen Darryn Peck drowning his parents in the creek.

I had the idea this morning while I was doing the eggs.

Why not have Amanda do the introduction in front of the tree where Darryn abandoned Sticky?

It seemed like a good idea at the time.

When Amanda arrived at the old shed she agreed.

'Good thinking,' she said. 'Kill two birds with one stone.'

I put my hands over Sticky's ears and gave her a look.

'Sorry,' she said.

When we got to the tree I climbed it with Sticky on my shoulder, put him on the branch, showed him the pictures, climbed down, focused the camera on Amanda and gave her a wave.

'This poor mistreated bird . . .' she said.

Then she stopped.

Sticky had flown down and was standing on her head.

Six times I climbed the tree with Sticky and six times he flew down.

The sixth time Amanda lost her temper.

'Get up that tree, banana-head, and stay there,' she yelled at Sticky, who was trying to undo her shoelaces with his beak.

Even though I was feeling pretty tense myself on account of Ms Dunning having a baby in three days and us not even having done the introduction yet, I tried to calm her down.

'He's just feeling nervous,' I said. 'He's had a scary experience here. It's like us going to the dentist.'

It was no good.

Amanda was looking in the other direction.

'I said get up that tree!' she yelled at Sticky.

Sticky bit her on the ankle.

She screamed, then picked up an apple and threw it at him.

Luckily she missed, because Sticky wasn't in any condition to duck.

He was just standing there, rigid with shock.

Like me.

Amanda realised what she'd done and looked pretty shocked herself.

Before any of us could move, a voice came from behind us.

'Watch yourself, Cosgrove,' it said. 'You can get five years for chucking Batts' apples.'

We spun round.

Darryn Peck was standing there, smirking.

'Wish I could stay,' he said, 'but I can't hang around here all day watching you mistreat wildlife, I've got a miniseries to make.'

And he ran off down the track laughing to himself.

For a minute I felt as if I was going to explode with frustration and shrivel up with embarrassment at the same time.

Then I recovered the power of thought.

'Come on,' I said to Amanda. 'After him. This is our chance to talk to him about his crimes on camera.'

It took us a while because Sticky wouldn't get into his bucket before Amanda apologised.

'Sorry,' said Amanda at last, dabbing at her ankle with a hanky.

Then Amanda wouldn't go until Sticky apologised.

'Eat soap,' said Sticky.

'That's his way of saying sorry,' I explained to Amanda, pushing her down the track in the direction Darryn had gone.

As we got close to the creek we could hear Darryn shouting.

We crouched down and peered through the bushes and saw him and Trent Webster and Doug Walsh and a couple of kids on the other side of the creek.

Darryn was sitting on the bank with his head

in his hands while Trent filmed him with his camera.

'My parents,' sobbed Darryn loudly, 'both drowned. Swept off the bank by a freak wave in the middle of a picnic. I begged them to wear floaties.'

'Life jackets,' said Doug, holding up an exercise book. 'In the script it says life jackets.'

'Stop being a smartarse,' Darryn hissed at him, 'and try to arrest me.'

Doug stepped forward, and Trent swung the camera around till it was pointing at him.

'Police,' said Doug, reading from the exercise book. 'We've found your parents' bodies and they've both got lumps of concrete tied to their feet.'

Darryn jumped up and pulled a plastic sword from his belt.

'You'll never take me alive,' he shouted.

Doug stared at the sword.

'It says a gun in the script,' he said.

'Shut up and fall into the water when I kill you,' Darryn hissed at him.

Amanda nudged me.

'Start the camera,' she said and then she was on her feet yelling across the creek at Darryn.

'Darryn Peck,' she shouted, 'is it true that you had a cockatoo for six years?'

Darryn paused with the sword raised above his head and looked across at us. So did the others.

I switched on the camera and struggled to get Darryn and Amanda in focus at the same time.

'Pig's bum,' shouted Darryn.

'Is it also true,' yelled Amanda, 'that you ditched the cocky for a poodle?'

'Go suck a turnip,' yelled Darryn and went back to chopping Doug Walsh into tiny pieces.

Amanda and I discussed crossing the creek so he'd have to answer the questions, but it gets pretty deep in places and Amanda didn't want to risk it with the camera and I didn't want to risk it with Sticky.

'I've got a better idea,' I said. 'Let's go to his place and wait for him to get back. That's what they do on telly. They chase people through the house with the camera going and out into the back yard and finally corner them near the veggie garden where they break down and confess.'

I could see Amanda was having trouble with my hand movements.

I wrote it out.

Amanda read it and nodded.

'OK Ro,' she said in a loud voice so Darryn could hear, 'let's go back to your place and do a nature documentary about woolly aphids.'

Then we set off for Darryn's.

We didn't get there.

Darryn's place is on the other side of town, but in the main street we ran into a problem.

Dad and Ms Dunning.

Just as we were passing the dry-cleaners and Amanda was in the middle of pointing out Mr Shapiro's new van to me and I was wondering if old dry-cleaning vans feel as bad about being dumped as cockies and kids do, I saw Dad and Ms Dunning coming out of the hardware store carrying a baby car seat.

Normally I'd have been pleased to see them, but not today.

Not when I was carrying a bucket with a cocky in it that I was meant to have given back to Darryn Peck four days ago.

Dad and Ms Dunning hadn't seen me, so I grabbed Amanda and dragged her across the street and into her dad's shop.

Both Amanda and Sticky were looking at me as though I was mental, so I explained the situation to them.

'It's just for a couple of minutes,' I said, 'till Dad and Ms Dunning have gone.'

Sticky seemed happy with that, but Amanda looked nervously around.

The shop was empty apart from the usual rows and piles of neatly-folded clothes.

We could hear Mr Cosgrove in the changing cubicles, telling a customer that grey-green was definitely this year's colour.

I put my hand on Amanda's arm and gave her a look.

'Relax,' it said, 'I haven't chucked a dessert for nearly a week.'

But that's not what was worrying Amanda.

'Dad doesn't like animals in the shop,' she said quietly, 'not since Ray Hempel's cattle dog tried to round up all the suede jackets.'

I put Sticky's bucket down behind a rack of moleskin pants, partly so Mr Cosgrove wouldn't see Sticky if he came out of the cubicles, and partly so Sticky wouldn't have to listen to himself being compared to a dog.

Cockatoos mustn't like moleskin pants.

Either that or metal buckets.

Because just as Mr Cosgrove came out of the changing area and saw me and started looking nervous, there was the sound of fencing wire being ripped and suddenly Mr Cosgrove had something to be even more nervous about.

Sticky, flying screeching around the shop.

Amanda screamed, Mr Cosgrove yelled, and

the customer, who was coming out of the cubicles doing up his pants, grabbed his briefcase and held it in front of his privates.

Sticky swooped down, snatched up a pair of orange and brown checked shorts from a table display, flew twice round the shop with them in his beak, and dropped them onto a pile of pink shirts.

'Stop that,' yelled Mr Cosgrove.

I could understand why he was so upset, I've never liked orange and pink together either.

Then Mr Cosgrove noticed that Amanda was holding the video camera.

'Switch it on,' he shouted at her. 'The insurance'll never believe us otherwise.'

I grabbed a towelling bathrobe and waited for Sticky to land so I could gather him up in it.

Sticky didn't land for quite a while, mostly because Mr Cosgrove kept throwing shoes at him and swiping at him with belts.

I pleaded with Amanda to get her dad to stop, but every time she tried to say something to him he yelled at her to keep on filming.

Sticky swooped round and round the shop, snatching up socks and ties and thermal underwear and knocking over piles of cardigans and footy tops.

By the time he finally landed on a rack of safari suits and I was able to get him into the bathrobe and then into the bucket and wire the chook mesh down securely, the shop was pretty untidy and Mr Cosgrove was an even brighter purple than Dad's wedding shirt.

'Your parents are gunna hear about this,' he roared as Amanda bundled me out of the shop.

'Don't worry,' Amanda said to me outside, 'he'll calm down once we get everything back in the right piles.'

I tried to be angry with Sticky on the way home, but I couldn't.

I glared at him a few times, and each time he went from mohawk to cowlick and looked down at the bottom of the bucket.

'This poor mistreated bird,' he said, 'has suffered.'

I was pretty impressed. It was quite a mouthful, even if he had heard it thirty or forty times.

But it didn't change the fact that we'll have to finish the in-depth report without him. We can't creep up on Darryn Peck's place tomorrow with a deranged cocky swooping around flinging washing and dog food all over the place.

'Fraid you'll have to stay put tomorrow,' I told Sticky as I shut him in his cage with fresh seed and water. 'It'll just be for one day.'

'I can't do it,' screeched Sticky. 'I resign.'

I felt awful as I walked to the house.

I still do.

I should have been more honest with Sticky. I should have explained that if Mr Cosgrove rings Dad before tomorrow, we're both in deep cocky poo.

But then what's the point in us both having a knot in our guts the size of Ayers Rock including the car park, the kiosk, the motel, the air strip and all the rubbish bins?

It's eight-thirty and he hasn't rung yet.

Dad's just been in to say goodnight and if Mr Cosgrove had rung I know Dad would have said more than, 'By the way, how's the telly project going?'

'OK,' I said.

I put my hands under the sheet.

'Has to be finished tomorrow, doesn't it?' he asked.

I nodded.

'Think you'll make it?' he asked.

I nodded.

'Good on you,' he said. 'Sounds like a top show, endangered wildlife. As long as you don't include codling moths.'

I smiled.

'G'night, Tonto,' said Dad. 'I've got to get back to Claire. She's teaching me how to fold nappies her way.'

That was ten minutes ago.

My hands are still under the sheet, fingers crossed so tightly they feel like cocky claws.

I burnt the eggs this morning.

It's the first time I've ever done it, and I could see it made Ms Dunning suspicious.

'Are you OK, Ro?' she asked, but it wasn't the tone of voice your dad's wife uses, it was the tone of voice a teacher uses when you're daydreaming and burning the chemicals in science.

Or the eggs.

'Sorry,' I said, blowing at the smoke, 'I was miles away.'

That was a slight exaggeration.

In my head I'd only been three metres away, over by the phone, waiting for it to ring and Mr Cosgrove to say that he wasn't letting Amanda use his video camera anymore and that he had the address of a really good home for uncontrollable cockies and kids.

Ms Dunning and Dad went back to their conversation about babies' names.

'Caroline,' said Ms Dunning.

'Carla,' said Dad.

'Amelia,' said Ms Dunning.

'Leanne,' said Dad.

'Lachlan,' said Ms Dunning.

'Clarrie,' said Dad.

'Our neighbours had a turtle called Clarrie,' said Ms Dunning.

'My dad's name was Clarrie,' said Dad.

'I'm not really hungry,' I said. 'Bye.'

As I left the house the phone still hadn't rung.

I decided Mr Cosgrove must still have been tidying up the shop.

I could hardly breathe by the time I got to the end of Darryn Peck's street in case Amanda wasn't there or was there but didn't have the camera.

She was there.

She had the camera.

'I reminded Dad you're a disadvantaged person,' said Amanda. 'Sorry.'

I gave her a hug.

Normally I'd have been ropeable, but sometimes you have to be lenient when a clever and generous best friend's trying to stop your life from going down the dunny.

Even if later the same day it ends up down there anyway.

Getting into Darryn Peck's place was easier today than it would have been six months ago because six months ago his three big brothers were still living at home and there was always at least one of them lying in the front yard under a motorbike with a spanner at all hours of the day and night.

This morning the front yard was empty except for a few bushes near the front door.

Me and Amanda went and crouched in them, camera and clipboard at the ready.

'He's definitely still in the house,' said Amanda, using her hands. 'I've been at the end of the street since six-thirty.'

She's incredible. She'll be on national television by the time she's twenty-three.

After I finished telling her that, we headed for the front door.

Then I had a thought.

'If he sees us ringing the bell,' I said, dragging Amanda back into the bushes, 'he could lock himself in the bathroom. We've got to take him by surprise. Round the back.'

We crept along the side of the house, ducking under the windows, and peered round the corner into the back yard.

Darryn's mother was kneeling at a small table just outside the back door, making strange noises.

'Oochy, oochy, oochy,' she went. 'Goo, goo, goo, goo, goo.'

It sounded like she was feeding a baby. I knew she hadn't had a baby recently, but for a sec I thought maybe she was feeding someone else's as a part-time job.

Then she moved a bit and I saw it wasn't a baby but the poodle, which was standing on the table looking bored while she combed its curls with a tiny comb.

'Who's a beautiful girl then?' cooed Mrs Peck.

The dog didn't answer, but I could see it eyeing Mrs Peck's hairdo, which was very similar to its own, and wishing it had a tiny comb too.

Then Mr Peck came out of the house and started making baby noises as well.

'Ga, ga, ga, ga, ga, ga, ga, ga, ga, ga,' said Mr Peck.

You don't often hear a forklift-truck operator talking like that.

I could feel Amanda shaking with silent laughter and I put my hand over her mouth just in case.

Mr Peck tilted the poodle's head up and pushed its legs a bit further apart. 'First prize,' he said, speaking into his fist, 'goes to Amelia Peck Hyloader The Third.'

Then me and Amanda stiffened.

Darryn was coming out of the house.

He stood watching his parents, shoulders drooping.

Then he took a deep breath and spoke.

'Dad,' he said, 'why can't we go to the cricket tomorrow? You promised.'

Mr Peck answered without looking up from the poodle. 'You know why,' he said. 'We've got Amelia in the show.'

Darryn's shoulders drooped even further. 'You've got her in a show every Saturday,' he said bitterly.

'Don't raise your voice to your father,' said Mrs Peck, not looking up either, 'it's making the dog nervous.'

Darryn looked at his parents for a moment and then turned and walked towards us.

We flattened ourselves against the fibro but he came round the corner with his head down and walked straight past us.

Amanda nudged me and headed after him. I switched the camera on and by the time they were halfway across the front lawn I had them both in focus.

'Darryn Peck,' said Amanda in her best reporter voice, 'is it true that you ditched your faithful cockatoo for a poodle?'

Darryn swung round.

'I hate that poodle,' he shouted, 'I've always hated it.'

Then he realised who he was talking to and froze.

That's when I saw the tears in his eyes.

Darryn Peck was crying.

I turned the camera off.

'But you did abandon a cockatoo,' persisted Amanda, before she felt me gripping her arm and saw Darryn's tears and realised it was time to shut up.

'Yeah, what of it?' Darryn said, but his heart wasn't in it.

He looked so helpless and unhappy I wanted to put my arms round him.

Then he took a step forward and for a sec I thought he was going to grab the camera and hurl it over the neighbour's fence.

Instead he turned and ran into the house.

Amanda and me looked at each other.

'We could do an in-depth report on Darryn's parents,' she said quietly.

I shook my head.

It wouldn't change anything.

We walked into town without saying much and when we got to school I gave her the camera and she gave me a hug and I set off for home.

I'm almost there.

I'm hurrying so I can see as much of Dad as possible in the little bit of time left before the baby's born, because afterwards I'm going to be pretty busy with the club.

The club I'm going to start.

It's got four members already.

Me, Sticky, Darryn Peck and Mr Shapiro's old van.

I could tell something was wrong as soon as I walked into the house.

Ms Dunning's Jelly Custard Surprise, the one she'd made for the Show, was sitting on the kitchen table without a flyscreen over it.

I knew she'd never leave it like that on purpose because everyone knows you can't win a prize in the Cakes And Puddings section if you've got fly footprints in your whipped cream.

Then Dad and Ms Dunning came into the kitchen and I could tell from their furious faces they had something more important on their minds than dessert.

For a while they just stood there glaring at me, and I realised they were struggling to control themselves.

By the time Dad finally spoke in a tight angry voice my heart was thumping faster than the fridge motor.

'I'm very disappointed in you, Ro,' he said.

'We're both very disappointed in you,' said Ms Dunning.

My mind was racing.

Had Mr Segal rung up asking why I wasn't at school?

Had Darryn gone out into the back yard and strangled the poodle and his parents were blaming me?

'We agreed you'd take that cockatoo back,' shouted Dad, 'didn't we?'

Ayers Rock hit me in the guts.

They'd found Sticky.

I started to ask if he was OK but the words froze on my hands.

Because I saw what Dad had on his hands.

Blood.

I couldn't believe it.

I'd seen him shoot at birds in the old days, before we had nets in the orchard, but now he's a big supporter of all the wildlife on the protected list.

Obviously poor old Sticky wasn't on his list.

Suddenly Ayers Rock wasn't in my guts any more, it was in my head and it had gone volcanic and I couldn't stop myself.

I erupted.

I wanted to shout and yell and scream, but all I could do was fling my hands around faster than I ever have before.

Hand movements might be hard to understand sometimes, but when they're that big and that fast everyone knows you're shouting.

'It's not fair!' I yelled. 'You're having a baby, why can't I have a cocky?'

Dad opened his mouth to answer but I hadn't finished.

'Why do you need a baby anyway?' I shouted. 'You've got me. What's wrong with me?'

Through my tears I saw Dad close his mouth.

'That's why you're having one, isn't it?' I yelled, banging my elbow on the fireplace. 'It's because there's something wrong with me. Isn't it? Isn't it?'

Dad and Ms Dunning were staring at me, stunned, so I thumped my fist down on the table to jolt them out of it.

The Jelly Custard Surprise wobbled.

I grabbed it and lifted it above my head and braced my legs to hurl it against the kitchen dresser as hard as I could.

But I didn't.

Because as Dad and Ms Dunning raised their hands in front of their faces I saw two things.

The blood on Dad's hands was coming from several small cuts on his palms and fingers.

And gripped in Ms Dunning's hands were several splinters of wood with bits of sleepy bunny on them.

Even as I pushed past Dad and Ms Dunning I knew what I'd find in the nursery. When I got in there it was even worse than I'd imagined.

The floor was littered with splintered pieces of bashful koala.

Torn shreds of playful dolphin were strewn over what was left of the baby's cot.

Frayed ribbons of friendly possum hung from the curtain rail.

The light shade was a tattered wreck with barely a scrap of goanna left that you'd recognise as being happy-go-lucky.

'That vicious cheese-brain tore the place apart,' shouted Dad furiously behind me, 'I tried to grab the brute but it pecked my hands and flew off.'

'It was in a frenzy,' said Ms Dunning.

'You've had it cooped up somewhere around here, haven't you?' demanded Dad.

I thrust the Jelly Custard Surprise at Dad and ran out of the house.

Dad shouted at me but as I ran down the verandah steps I heard Ms Dunning telling him to let me go.

I didn't care.

All I wanted was to find Sticky.

I went to the old shed but the cage was empty and a panel of chook-wire fencing was hanging loose. I kicked it and said some rude things in my head about people who spend so much money on baby things that they haven't got enough left over to buy decent cocky-proof tying wire.

Then I went looking for Sticky.

That was hours ago.

I've been all through the orchard and all round the creek and up the tree where I first found him and halfway into town.

I couldn't call his name of course so I had to make do with rattling some seed in his tin.

Pretty hopeless, because anyone can rattle seed in a tin.

Darryn Peck or Dad or Mr Cosgrove, with an apple or a gun or a noose made from a tape measure behind their back.

No wonder I couldn't find him.

He's probably migrated to Indonesia or Sulawesi or somewhere.

So I've just been sitting here, in his cage, looking at the remains of the pictures I drew him.

I really loved that cocky, even though he chewed everything up.

I haven't felt this lonely since Erin died. She was my best friend at the special school I used to go to and she was crook a lot but it was still a terrible shock when she died.

I felt pretty bad then too, but at least then I had a dad who really loved me.

I thought I'd managed to sneak into bed without being spotted but Dad came in.

I kept my head under the pillow but I knew it was him because he flicks his belt buckle with his thumbnail when he's nervous.

Or angry.

He stood there for ages without saying anything.

I guessed he wasn't angry any more. When Dad's angry you always know about it. At least he and Sticky had one thing in common.

Dad still didn't say anything.

For a moment I thought he was pausing for effect like he usually does before announcing a big surprise, but he wasn't.

When he finally spoke it wasn't 'We're having the baby adopted', it was 'Tonto, are you awake?'

I didn't move.

He went out.

In the old days, before his head was full of new ways to fold nappies, he'd have asked at least twice.

Then Ms Dunning came in.

I knew it was her because when she sat down the bed springs sagged violently. They're fine with one person on them but not three.

I kept my head under the pillow.

She didn't ask if I was awake, but that was probably because she's a teacher. Teachers always assume you'll be awake once they start talking.

'Ro,' she said, 'I've got something to tell you. Dad wasn't sure if you should know this, but I think you should.'

She paused.

I held my breath.

Teachers must do training in how to grab your attention without using loud music or explosive devices.

'But first, Ro,' Ms Dunning said, 'we're not trying to replace you. We'd never do that.'

I stuck my hands out from under the sheet and made the sign me and Dad invented for a defective apple.

Ms Dunning put her hands over mine.

'You're not defective,' she said. 'You've got a speech problem you handle like a champ and if the baby's born with a similar speech problem I know it'll handle it like a champ too.'

That got me out from under the pillow.

I rolled over and stared at Ms Dunning.

A similar speech problem?

The baby?

For a sec I thought Ms Dunning was having another vague spell and had got her words mixed up, but then I saw from the expression on her face that she hadn't.

'It's possible,' she said. 'The doctors have never told you this, but they reckon they know why you were born mute.'

I stared at her even harder.

I'd asked the doctors that a million times and each time they'd said I was a Medical Mystery and given me a lolly.

'They reckon,' continued Ms Dunning, 'it's because of some genetic problem that's been in either your dad's family or your mum's family for generations. They don't know which.'

My brain was going like a GT Falcon with twin injectors.

If it was Dad's that would explain why he'd never told me.

If I was him I'd be too embarrassed to yak on about something like that as well.

'If it's a problem on Dad's side,' Ms Dunning went on, 'then the baby could be born mute too.'

We looked at each other for a while.

I didn't know what to say.

Ms Dunning looked pretty sad.

She leant over and kissed me on the cheek. 'We decided to tell you because we want you to feel better,' she murmured. Then she went out.

I've been lying here for a long time, staring into the darkness.

I've been thinking how, if the baby's born mute, I can help it.

Teach it sign language.

Show it how to write really fast so it can get its order in to the school tuck shop before all the devon and chutney sandwiches are gone.

Demonstrate what you have to do with your nose when you're cheering your best friend up with a look.

I've also been thinking what great parents I've got.

Well, good parents.

Well, their hearts are in the right place.

Even though I brandished a Jelly Custard Surprise at them in the kitchen and my pet cocky murdered all their sleepy bunnies, they still want me to feel better.

I know I should feel better, but I don't.

Because even dads with hearts in the right place are only human.

And if that baby talks, what chance have I got?

It's a funny thing, the human brain.

I don't mean to look at, though I saw one in a jar once in a museum and it did look a bit weird, like scrambled eggs when you don't wash the mushroom juice out of the pan first.

I mean the way it works.

When I woke up this morning I decided I'd spend the day helping Dad and Ms Dunning clean up the baby's room.

While I was getting dressed I had the thought that if we pulled the old shed apart and sanded the wood we could probably build some pretty good baby furniture out of it.

While I was tying my left shoe I remembered my softball bat. We could sell that and use the money to buy blue and pink paint.

Then, while I was tying my right shoe, I forgot about all those things totally and completely.

Because I started thinking about Darryn Peck.

I was sitting on the bed bending over, so perhaps the blood sloshing around in my head made my brain short-circuit or something.

Or perhaps I was just trying to take my mind off Sticky.

Anyway once I started thinking about him I couldn't stop.

I thought about how Darryn and me are in the same boat.

I thought about the poodle.

I thought about how much easier it'd be to compete with two kilos of curly fluff and a squeaky bark than with a kid who'll probably be singing opera by the age of three.

I thought about how I wished I could swap places with Darryn, and what I'd do if I was in his shoes, and how he'd probably never think of doing the same because he's not real bright.

Then I thought about him crying and my guts felt strange and I don't think it was because I hadn't had any dinner.

Dad and Ms Dunning were still asleep.

I wrote them a note, left it on the kitchen table, grabbed a couple of cold apple fritters from the fridge and slipped out of the house.

On my way into town I thought about how weird the human brain is.

There I was, on what was possibly my last morning ever as a single kid, walking away from possibly my last ever morning cuddle with Dad without some noisy brat yodelling in our ears and dribbling on his shirt.

Just to save Darryn Peck from a life of misery.

It was still early when I reached town and the main street was almost deserted. Just a couple of shopkeepers hosing the footpath and Mr Shapiro polishing his new van.

He called me over.

I hesitated, wondering if he was going to hand me a bill for burnt-out dry-cleaning machines, but he smiled and beckoned.

'Good on you, love,' he said, and gave me two dollars.

I spent it in the newsagents on a new notepad and pen because getting through to Darryn Peck can involve a lot of writing. Particularly when he's still ropeable about being ambushed with a camera and sprung with tears in his eyes.

When I got to Darryn's place I rang the bell and stood there holding up the first note.

'Don't do anything violent,' it said, 'until you've read this note. I'm here to help you avoid a life of misery. There will be no charge for this service.'

Darryn opened the door in his pyjamas.

He stared at me, ignoring the note completely, and took a menacing step towards me.

'You can't have him,' he said.

I took a step back, wondering what he was talking about.

Then I heard a distant voice and I knew.

'Go suck a turnip,' said the voice.

I pushed past Darryn and ran through the house, past a startled Mr and Mrs Peck who were at the kitchen table shampooing the poodle.

I burst out of the back door and there in the corner of the yard was a big cage and sitting on a branch in one corner calling me a big fat wobbly bottom was Sticky.

Darryn ran past me and into the cage and grabbed Sticky off his perch and held him tightly.

'He's mine,' said Darryn fiercely.

'You dumped him,' I scribbled on my pad, just as fiercely.

'Darryn,' shouted his father from the back door, 'if you're letting that bird out keep it away from Amelia.'

Darryn's face sagged.

'I only dumped him for them,' he said, nodding towards the kitchen. 'I reckoned things might be better if they thought I was shifting over to poodles.'

He looked bitterly towards the kitchen.

'Fat chance,' he said.

'Darryn,' shouted his father, 'Amelia's having a sleep on your bed. Don't disturb her.'

Darryn gave Sticky a hug.

'I should never have done it,' he said sadly. 'But Sticky's forgiven me, haven't you mate.'

'Drop off a log,' said Sticky.

'See,' said Darryn, beaming, 'he's talking to me now.'

He gave Sticky another hug and I had to admit it did look as though Sticky had forgiven him. He wasn't shredding Darryn's ears or anything.

For a sec I was tempted to grab Sticky and run for it and hide out for a couple of years, just him and me, on a deserted island off the Philippines, but I decided against it.

Sticky gave me a look. 'Thanks for everything,' it said, 'but I'm home now.'

Darryn let me have a couple of private minutes with Sticky to say goodbye.

We both got pretty moist in the eyes, Sticky and me, and while I was showing him a picture of me coming to visit him often, and he was telling me to bite my bum, I made a promise to myself that one day I'll have a cocky all of my own.

It occurred to me, as Darryn was putting Sticky back into the cage, that Ms Dunning had probably felt the same way about having a baby.

Then I took Darryn for a long walk and wrote him lots of notes and slowly he grasped my plan to save him from a life of misery.

He was a bit doubtful at first, but when we got here to the showground he realised what a great plan it is.

Everything's set up, Darryn's in position, people have started arriving, and we're just waiting now for the mayor to declare the Agricultural Show open.

The plan didn't work.

I still can't believe it.

Everything went as smoothly as a well-oiled apple-polishing machine and the plan still didn't work.

I waited till the judging had started in the Dog tent, then I wheeled the extra display stand in.

Mr and Mrs Peck were so busy fussing about with their poodle that they didn't notice me getting into position next to them at the end of the row of dogs.

I timed it spot on.

Just as the judges were inspecting Amelia Peck Hyloader The Third, I whipped the cover off my stand.

The judges moved on, peered over their clipboards, and the blood drained from their faces.

It was probably the first time they'd seen a boy on a dog display stand.

Darryn was brilliant.

He panted and got up on all fours and looked at his parents with mournful eyes and let his tongue loll out.

He looked exactly like a boy whose parents treat him worse than a dog.

That's when everything went wrong.

Mr and Mrs Peck didn't sweep him up in their arms and weep and say how sorry they were and promise never to boot him out of his room again when the poodle wanted a nap.

They didn't even look at each other and say, 'Let this be a lesson to us not to neglect Darryn in future'.

Mrs Peck just screamed.

And Mr Peck just shouted, 'Darryn, get off there this minute, you're upsetting the dogs'.

Darryn was very good about it all.

After we'd run for it and hidden behind the Jam And Preserves tent and seen that no one was following us, he thanked me.

'It was a good try,' he said sadly.

Then he went off to find his mates.

I felt awful.

I wrote a long note explaining that it was all my idea and that Darryn shouldn't be punished because he'd only agreed to do it because he was gullible, and I left it under the Pecks' windscreen wiper.

Walking back across the car park I was spotted by the one person I didn't want to be spotted by.

Mr Segal.

'Rowena,' he called out, 'about your TV project.'

It was too late to run.

Mr Segal sprinted over and blocked my way.

'Brilliant,' he said, breaking into a grin, 'I haven't laughed so much for ages.'

It took me a while to grasp what he was saying because I couldn't take my eyes off the dinosaurs on his shirt.

I stared at him and tried to smile back.

'You and Amanda have got a big future in TV comedy,' he said. 'Well done.'

I found Amanda over by the sheep and cattle enclosure.

She explained that because ten seconds of Darryn Peck crying wasn't really enough for an in-depth current affairs report, she'd handed in the tape of Sticky flying round the menswear shop and her dad throwing shoes at him.

'Mr Segal wants to show it at a video festival,' Amanda said excitedly. 'Pretty good eh?'

I said it wasn't bad, but that I wasn't really in the mood for celebrating.

Amanda, because she's a true friend, didn't pester me for details, she just squeezed my arm and we went over to the stand to find a good position for the Carla Tamworth concert.

As we passed the Cakes And Puddings tent I saw a familiar hat weaving towards us through the crowd and my heart started thumping like a Saint Bernard's tail.

It was Dad.

He'd come to see the concert with me after all.

We ran towards him, me waving like a loon, until I saw what he was carrying.

A Jelly Custard Surprise.

'Can't stop,' he said, 'it's melting,' and he hurried into the Cakes And Puddings tent.

I stared after him and blinked hard.

He was just dropping off Ms Dunning's entry.

Amanda took my arm and we found a good pozzie halfway up the stand.

There was a support band playing a song about a person whose heart had been run over by a steamroller, which was pretty right for the way I was feeling.

Then a ripple of alarm ran through the crowd.

People started craning to see.

There was some sort of commotion.

Up on the stage someone seemed to be having a heated discussion with the lead singer of the support band.

My guts froze.

I recognised the purple shirt and the white hat with the tractor exhaust stains.

It was Dad.

'It's your dad,' yelled Amanda, who'd obviously forgotten she was meant to be a true friend.

People turned round and stared at me and I wanted to hide under the seat, but it was just a bench and there wasn't room.

The lead singer of the support band stepped up to the microphone shaking his head.

'One of your local blokes wants to sing,' he said, 'and because he's a pushy so and so we've decided to let him.'

The support band filed off the stage leaving Dad standing at the mike by himself.

Dad cleared his throat.

'I'd like to sing a little number I wrote myself,' he said.

I couldn't believe it.

Dad didn't write songs.

Even as Dad was clearing his throat again, people started throwing things.

Chip cartons.

Cigarette packets.

Bottle tops.

A couple of people yelled out to give him a go, and the rest of us just sat there stunned that anyone would try and sing to a crowd of this size without a guitar.

Dad started singing and a lot more people started throwing things.

Beer cans.

Ice creams.

Bits of hot dog.

It was the worst I'd ever heard him sing.

He was off key and none of the lyrics rhymed.

But I didn't care.

Because Dad stood there ignoring the food and garbage raining down on him and the crowd yelling 'Jump off a cliff' and 'Take a hike' and 'Get stuffed', and sang to me.

He didn't take his eyes off me the whole time he sang, and I didn't take mine off him.

Part of me wanted to yell at the crowd to shut

up, but the other part of me was too busy glowing like a two-million-watt bulb.

The song was about a girl who's lived most of her life without a mother and so her father decides to give her the most precious gift he can think of.

A brother or sister.

When he'd finished, and the crowd had all booed, and I'd wiped my tears away, I wanted to jump up on my seat and cheer my lungs out.

I couldn't of course, and it took Amanda about a minute to stop looking dazed and do it, and during that time I found myself thinking how you never have a kid sister or brother with a good cheering voice around when you need one.

Then I ran down to the stage and Dad, who was splattered with beer and ice cream and bits of hot dog, hugged me so tight he left a red mark just above my bellybutton.

It wasn't his belt buckle, it was tomato sauce.

'I'd better ring home,' said Dad, 'see if the baby's coming.'

I couldn't have agreed more.

As we hurried to the pay phone we passed the Cake And Pudding tent.

I glanced inside, and across the heads of all the people, over in one corner, in front of the big hardware store fan, I was sure I saw Darryn Peck with Ms Dunning's Jelly Custard Surprise raised above his head.

We made it to the hospital just in time.

Dad sat me in the waiting room and gave me some money for the drink machine and hurried through the swing doors with Ms Dunning.

It was a long wait.

I had a drink every half hour and tried to ignore a little kid with blonde hair who kept pointing to me and saying to her dad, 'There's something wrong with her'.

I almost strangled her a couple of times, but spent the rest of the time straining to hear something.

Anything.

Then Dad appeared flushed and red-eyed and grinning and took me inside to a ward.

Ms Dunning was sitting up in bed.

She was flushed and red-eyed and grinning too.

Lying on her chest was a small wrinkled baby.

It wasn't making a sound.

Come on, I said inside, come on.'

'This is your sister,' said Dad in a wobbly voice. 'Her name's Erin.'

Even when I heard that I didn't stop holding my breath, not until Erin opened her mouth and gave a howl that rattled the windows.

Then I realised I was bawling my eyes out, but it didn't matter because Dad and Ms Dunning were too.

After a while, when we'd pulled ourselves together, and I was holding Erin, I noticed that the little blonde kid had wondered in, probably attracted by the noise Erin was making.

'Look,' said the kid to a nurse, 'the girl that's got something wrong with her, she's picked up that baby.'

I turned and spoke to her.

I knew she was too young to understand hand movements, but I wanted to say it.

'This is my sister,' I said, 'and there's nothing wrong with either of us.'

Morris Gleitzman
Blabber Mouth

Two hours ago, when I walked into this school for the first time, the sun was shining, the birds were singing, and, apart from a knot in my guts the size of Tasmania, life was great. Now here I am, locked in a stationery cupboard. I wish those teachers would stop shouting at me to come out.

Hiding in cupboards is one way of dealing with your problems. Especially when you've just stuffed a frog into Darryn Peck's mouth.

But Rowena Batts has a bigger problem. Her dad. How can she tell him that his shirts, and his singing voice, are wrecking her life? It's not easy – especially when you can't speak . . .

'A wonderful novel' SCHOOL LIBRARIAN

'Hysterically funny' BOOKS FOR KEEPS

Morris Gleitzman
Misery Guts

Keith's heart was pounding. Calm down, he thought. You're not robbing a bank. You're not kidnapping anybody. You're just painting a fish and chip shop orange.

Keith is trying to cheer up his parents. But a pair of misery guts need more than a pot of Tropical Mango Hi-Gloss to make them happy. What they really need, Keith decides, is to live in Paradise.

Trouble is, Paradise is halfway round the world.

Even Keith Shipley is stumped by that one. Almost.

'Totally compelling' CHILDREN'S BOOKS OF THE YEAR

'Great fun' BOOKS FOR KEEPS

Morris Gleitzman
Worry Warts

Dear Mum and Dad,

This is just to let you know that I took the torch, the hammer, the gardening trowel, the plastic strainer, the chocolate biscuits and the stuff that's missing from the bathroom. So it's OK, you haven't been burgled. Please don't worry, things are looking even better than I thought, opal-wise.

Love, Keith

Going down a mine and digging up a fortune in precious opals is Keith's solution to his parents' problems. Stacks of money will make everything OK in their tropical paradise, and save them from being permanent worry warts.

Won't it?

Another brilliant Keith Shipley plan – if it works . . .

Morris Gleitzman
Two Weeks with the Queen

Dear Your Majesty the Queen,

I need to speak to you urgently about my brother Luke. He's got cancer and the doctors in Australia are being really slack. If I could borrow your top doctor for a few days I know he/she would fix things up in no time. Of course Mum and Dad would pay his/her fares even if it meant selling the car or getting a loan. Please contact me at the above address urgently.

Yours sincerely

Colin Mudford

P.S. This is not a hoax. Ring the above number and Aunty Iris will tell you. Hang up if a man answers.

If you want something done properly – go straight to the top!

Getting the Queen to help won't be easy. But if she can't help – who can?

'One of the best books I've ever read. It's funny, moving and it handles difficult subjects with skill and great respect. I'm glad I read it. I wish that I had written it.' Paula Danziger

'A remarkably exciting, moving and funny book.'
CHILDREN'S BOOKS OF THE YEAR 1989

'A marvellous book – funny and wise.'
BOOKS FOR KEEPS

'A gem of a book.'
Stephanie Netall, THE GUARDIAN

A selected list of titles available from Macmillan and Pan Books

The prices shown below are correct at the time of going to press. However, Macmillan Publishers reserve the right to show new retail prices on covers which may differ from those previously advertised.

All Macmillan titles can be ordered at your local bookshop or are available by post from:

**Book Service by Post
PO Box 29, Douglas, Isle of Man IM99 1BQ**

Credit cards accepted. For details:
Telephone: 01624 675137
Fax: 01624 670923
E-mail: bookshop@enterprise.net

Free postage and packing in the UK.
Overseas customers: add £1 per book (paperback)
and £3 per book (hardback).